T-Mac cleared his throat. "Since you don't need me, I'll go."

Kinsley's eyes flew open. "Do you have to?"

He shrugged. "No. My buddies are covering for me with my commander."

She held out her hand. "I think they gave me a sedative. Could you stay until I go to sleep?" Her lips twisted. "You don't have to if you don't want to."

He chuckled. "Playing second fiddle to a dog isn't quite a compliment, but I'll take it."

T-Mac pulled the chair close and gathered her hand in his, reveling at how small it was in his, yet how strong and supple her fingers were.

Agar leaned his long snout over Kinsley's body, sniffed T-Mac's hand once and then laid his head back on Kinsley's other side, seemingly satisfied T-Mac wouldn't harm the dog handler.

For a long moment, she said nothing.

T-Mac assumed she was sleeping.

"Don't tell anyone," Kinsley whispered, her eyes closed, her breathing slow and steady.

T-Mac stroked the back of her hand. "Tell anyone what?"

"That the tough-as-nails army soldier needed to hold a navy SEAL's hand."

SIX MINUTES
TO MIDNIGHT

New York Times Bestselling Author

ELLE JAMES

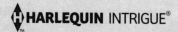

I'd like to dedicate this book to the military working dogs, who
are such an important addition to our fighting forces. They are
loyal, smart and dedicated to doing what they do best. Friends of
mine adopted a retired military working dog, which gave me the
idea to include him in this book. Agar, thanks for your service!

ISBN-13: 978-1-335-60410-1

Six Minutes to Midnight

Copyright © 2018 by Mary Jernigan

Recycling programs
for this product may
not exist in your area.

HARLEQUIN®
™ www.Harlequin.com

Printed in U.S.A.

Elle James, a *New York Times* bestselling author, started writing when her sister challenged her to write a romance novel. She has managed a full-time job and raised three wonderful children, and she and her husband even tried ranching exotic birds (ostriches, emus and rheas). Ask her, and she'll tell you what it's like to go toe-to-toe with an angry 350-pound bird! Elle loves to hear from fans at ellejames@earthlink.net or ellejames.com.

Visit the Author Profile page at Harlequin.com.

CAST OF CHARACTERS

"T-Mac" Trace McGuire—US Navy SEAL, communications man, equipment expert.

Specialist Kinsley Anderson—US Army, dog handler.

Sergeant Agar—German shepherd, US Army military working dog.

"Buck" Graham Buckner—US Navy SEAL, team medic. Went to medical school but didn't finish. Joined the navy and became a SEAL.

"Diesel" Dalton Samuel Landon—US Navy SEAL. Gunner and team lead.

"Pitbull" Percy Taylor—US Navy SEAL. Tough guy who doesn't date much. Raised by a taciturn marine father. Lives by the rules and structure. SOC-R boat captain.

"Harm" Harmon Payne—US Navy SEAL. For a big guy, he's light on his feet and fast. Good at silent entry into buildings.

"Big Jake" Schuler—US Navy SEAL, demolitions expert. Big guy with a big heart he's afraid to give to any one woman. His job as a SEAL is his life.

William Toland—Construction contractor.

Reese Brantley—Medically retired from active duty with the US Army, veteran of mixed martial arts fighting, now a bodyguard for hire in the DC area.

Alexandria "Alex" Parker—Teacher living with a missionary family. She came for the adventure and to teach village children and orphans.

Dr. Angela Vega—Provided medical care for people in South Sudan with Doctors Without Borders. Now working in Bethesda, Maryland, at Walter Reed Medical Center.

Marly Simpson—Former bush pilot in Africa, now flying charter in the Virginia and Washington, DC, area. Her father was a bush pilot in Africa and taught her to fly.

Talia Montclair—Former owner/operator of the All Things Wild Resort in Kenya.

Chapter One

"Four days and a wakeup," Trace McGuire, T-Mac to his friends, said as he sat across the table in the chow hall on Camp Lemonnier. They'd returned from their last mission in Niger with news they were scheduled to redeploy back to the States.

He glanced around the table at his friends. When they were deployed, they spent practically every waking hour together. In the past, being stateside was about the same. They'd go to work, train, get briefed, work out and then go back to their apartments. Most of the time, they'd end up at one of the team members' places to watch football, cook out or just lounge around and shoot the crap with each other. They were like family and never seemed to get tired of each other's company.

T-Mac suspected all that was about to change. All of his closest SEAL buddies had women in their lives now. All except him. Suddenly, going back to Virginia wasn't quite as appealing as it had been in the past. T-Mac sighed and drank his lukewarm coffee.

"I can't wait to see Reese." Diesel tapped a finger against the rim of his coffee cup. "I promised to take her on a real date when I get back to civilization."

"What? You're not going to take her swinging through the jungle, communing with the gorillas?" Buck teased.

Petty Officer Dalton Samuel Landon, otherwise known as Diesel, shook his head. "Nope. Been there, done that. I think I'll take her to a restaurant where we don't have to forage for food. Then maybe we'll go out to a nightclub." He tipped his head to the side. "I wonder if she likes to dance."

"You mean you don't know?" Big Jake Schuler, the tallest man on the team, rolled his eyes. "I would have thought that in the time you two spent traipsing along the Congo River, you would know everything there was to know about each other."

Diesel frowned. "I know what's important. She's not fragile, she can climb a tree when she needs to, she doesn't fall apart when someone's shooting at her and she can kiss like nobody's business." Diesel shrugged. "In fact, I'm looking forward to learning more. She's amazing. How many female bodyguards do you know?"

Big Jake held up his hands in surrender. "You got me there. None."

"I can't wait to see Angela." Corpsman Graham "Buck" Buckner, the team medic, smiled. "She's interviewing for positions around Little Creek."

"With her doctor credentials, and the work she

did with Doctors Without Borders, she's sure to get on pretty quickly," Big Jake said. "If not one of the military hospitals, there are lots of civilian hospitals and clinics in the area."

Buck nodded. "I can't believe after all these years, she'd want to be close to me." He smiled. "I'm one lucky guy."

"Yeah, and maybe she'll talk you into going back to school to finish your medical degree." Built solid like a tank, Percy Taylor had the tenacity of a pit bull, thus his nickname, Pitbull. He gave Buck a chin lift. "You'd make a good doc."

"What?" Buck spread his arms wide. "And give up all this?"

T-Mac chuckled. "I know. It's hard to believe anyone would want to stop being on call at all hours of the day and night, deploying to some of the worst hellholes on the planet and not getting back to see your family for months on end. Who would want to give up all that?"

"Hey, are we getting cynical in our old age?" Harmon Payne clapped a hand on T-Mac's back. "We're the ones who are going to suffer. We all have women to come home to now."

"All except T-Mac," Buck pointed out. "Maybe we should fix him up with someone? You think one of our women knows someone who could put up with his being a computer nerd and all?"

T-Mac shook his head. "I don't need help getting a date, thank you very much."

"I'll bet Reese has met some pretty hot chicks in the DC area through her work as a bodyguard," Diesel said. "Or maybe she still has some connections in the mixed-martial-arts community. One of those women are bound to be able to stand toe-to-toe with our guy."

"Seriously." T-Mac pushed to his feet. "I don't need a woman in my life. You all know how hard our lives are without relationships. I'm surprised all you self-confirmed bachelors broke the cardinal rule."

Pitbull stabbed the mystery meat on his tray with his fork and held it in the air, inspecting it with a frown. "What cardinal rule?"

T-Mac pounded his fist on the table. "Don't get into a permanent relationship as long as you're a full-time SEAL."

"Nope." Harm's eyes narrowed and his lips twisted. "I don't remember that line in the BUD/S training manual."

"Before we came to Africa," T-Mac reminded them, "we were drinking beer and talking about how we didn't have wives and kids—"

"Ha!" Pitbull held up a finger. "We were drinking beer. That's where we got off track."

Swallowing his irritation, T-Mac continued. "We all agreed that relationships were doomed to failure as long as we were doing the jobs we do. No woman will be satisfied being on a part-time status, what with us shipping out as often as we do to fight some battle nobody else wants."

"Then I found Marly," Pitbull said. "She can stand on her own two feet. And we get along pretty well." He smiled, his rugged face softening. "She's even getting me to like flying in crop dusters. And she's found a charter company in Virginia that wants her to pilot for them. She won't be waiting around for me to come home. Hell, we'll be lucky to be home at the same time."

"Exactly," T-Mac said. "And how's that going to work for you? You won't see each other."

Pitbull frowned. "We'll find time." His frown turned upside down. "And when we do…yup." He nodded. "We'll find time. I'm not ready to give up on her, and I don't think she'll give up on me."

"The point you're missing, T-Mac, is that we found women who can stand on their own," Harm said. "They don't need us any more than we need them. We *want* to be together. And that makes all the difference."

"Uh-huh." T-Mac knew they wouldn't listen. His five friends were so besotted by their women, they couldn't see past the rose-colored glasses to reality. He might as well save his breath.

"Guys." Buck stared around the table at everyone but T-Mac and lowered his voice to a conspiratorial whisper. "We've got to get T-Mac laid. He's strung way too tight. He's likely to blow a gasket soon."

"What's the use?" T-Mac pushed to his feet. "We're headed home in four days. Let's not screw anything up between now and then."

"What could possibly go wrong?" Buck asked with a grin and then ducked as everyone else threw their napkins and food at him.

Pitbull snorted. "Thanks for jinxing us, dirtbag."

"You guys can hang around talking about your women you'll rarely see. I'm going for a run." T-Mac walked out of the chow hall to the laughter of his friends.

"Gotta get him a girl," Buck said.

As T-Mac rounded the corner of one of the stacks of shipping containers that had been outfitted to become sleeping quarters, a hard object landed at his feet.

He jumped back, his heart racing, his first thought *Grenade!* Then a hair missile barreled toward him, all four legs moving like a blur.

T-Mac braced himself for impact.

The black-faced, sable German shepherd skidded to a stop, pushing up a cloud of dust in the process. He grabbed the object in his teeth and raced back the way he'd come.

"Agar, heel!" a female voice commanded.

The animal stopped immediately at the female soldier's side, dropped the hard rubber object on the ground and stared up at the woman as if eagerly awaiting the next command.

"Good dog." She patted him on the head and then glanced up. "Sorry. I didn't know you were there until after I'd thrown his KONG." Her hand continued to stroke the dog's head.

T-Mac stared at the woman, who was wearing camouflage pants, boots and a desert-tan T-shirt. Her hair was pulled back in a bun that had long since lost its shape. Coppery red strands danced in the breeze. She returned his stare with a direct green-eyed gaze. "If you're afraid of Agar, I'll hold him while you pass." She cocked an auburn eyebrow.

"What?" T-Mac shook his head. "I'm not afraid of the dog. Just startled."

"Then don't let us keep you." She snapped the lead on the dog's collar and straightened.

Curiosity made T-Mac ask, "You're new at Camp Lemonnier?"

She shrugged. "I've been here a week, if you consider that new."

He laughed. "I do. And I just got back to camp, or I'm sure I'd have seen you." There weren't too many good-looking redheaded females in the world, much less in Djibouti. "Hi, I'm Petty Officer Trace McGuire. My friends call me T-Mac." He took a step forward, slowly so as not to alert the dog, and held out his hand.

She clasped it in a firm grip. "Specialist Kinsley Anderson." She glanced down at the dog. "And this is Sergeant Agar."

T-Mac dropped to one knee in front of the German shepherd and held out his hand.

Agar placed a paw in his palm.

With a chuckle, T-Mac shook the dog's paw and then stood. "He's very well trained. What's his mission?"

"Bomb sniffing."

"Bomb sniffing?" T-Mac glanced again at the woman. He hadn't really thought about females on the front line. But with the army graduating females from Ranger School, it was a natural progression.

"Well, I hope you don't have to put that skill to use anytime soon."

Her eyes narrowed and she lifted her chin. "We came here to do a job. I'm not afraid."

Having seen his share of action and lost members of his team to gunfire and explosions, T-Mac didn't wish any of it on anyone. But a person had to live through the horrors of war to truly understand how terrible it was. He couldn't begin to explain it to the shiny new specialist who'd probably never been shot at or stood next to a man who'd been blown away by an IED.

And he had no business chatting up a female soldier when fraternization was strictly forbidden on deployment. Especially since it could lead to nothing and he and his team would be shipping out in four sleeps and a wakeup. "Well, it was nice to meet you."

"Same," she said, then grabbed the KONG and took off with Agar in the opposite direction.

As T-Mac continued on toward his quarters, he couldn't help sighing. He'd never considered dating a redhead, but something about Specialist Anderson made him reconsider. Perhaps it was the way her coppery hair seemed out of control, or the light dusting of freckles across her nose and cheeks. Or maybe it was the way she absently, or automatically, stroked the dog's head, showing it affection without having to think about it. Either way, she was off-limits and he was leaving. Once again he reminded himself, *Don't get involved*.

KINSLEY HURRIED PAST the navy guy. She'd spent the past two hours working with Agar, keeping his skills fresh and helping him burn off energy. Now it was her turn.

Though she'd been in the country for a week, she and Agar had been tasked only with inspecting vehicles entering Camp Lemonnier. Thankfully, they hadn't found any carrying explosives. Training sessions were a must, or Agar might forget what he was looking for and Kinsley might not pick up on the behavior Agar displayed when he sensed he'd found something.

Meanwhile, her male counterpart had gone out on missions with the Special Operations Forces into more hostile environments, working ahead of the teams to clear their routes of IEDs.

Kinsley had signed on as a dog handler because she loved dogs and because she wanted to make a difference for her country and her brothers in arms.

Her heart contracted as she thought about one in particular. Cody, her best friend from high school, had been killed in Iraq when he'd stepped on a mine.

Kinsley wanted to keep other young military men and women from the same fate.

On her first deployment, she'd hoped to land in Afghanistan or Iraq. Instead she'd landed in Djibouti, a fairly stable environment but also a jumping-off point to other more volatile areas. She hoped that her being female wouldn't keep them from mobilizing her to support missions outside the safety of the camp's borders.

Kinsley reached her quarters, filled a bowl full of water for Agar and stripped out of her uniform pants and boots. While Agar greedily slurped the entire contents of the bowl, Kinsley slipped on her army-issue PT shorts and running shoes and switched her desert-tan T-shirt for her army PT shirt. After strapping her flourescent belt around her waist and pulling her hair back into a ponytail, she planted a black army ball cap on her head and stepped out the door, leash in hand.

She moved smartly, walking past the rows of shipping-container quarters and other buildings, working her way through the complex toward the open field designated for PT.

She passed the motor pool and offices set aside for contractors who were providing additional support and building projects for the camp.

A silver-haired man stood at the corner of one of the buildings, smoking a cigarette. He wore khaki slacks and a polo shirt, incongruous with the multitude of uniforms from all branches of the military.

As she approached, he smiled. "Good afternoon," he said.

Not wanting to be rude, Kinsley slowed, though she'd rather speed by without engaging. "Hello."

He stepped in front of her. "You're new to the camp?"

"Yes, sir." She frowned, her gaze running over his civilian clothing. "I'm sorry, I don't think we've met." She held out her hand. "Specialist Anderson."

"William Toland." He reached out and shook her hand. "No, we haven't met. I'd remember a woman and her dog."

Kinsley's hand automatically dropped to Agar's head. "Sergeant Agar is a Military Working Dog."

"I assumed he was." The man reached out as if to pet the dog.

Agar's lips pulled back in a snarl and he growled low in his chest.

Toland snatched back his hand. "Not very friendly?"

Kinsley stepped between Agar and Toland. "He wasn't trained to be friendly. He's trained to sniff out explosives, not to be petted by strangers."

"Handy skill to have in a war." Toland stepped back. "And message received."

Kinsley nodded toward the construction crane at the far end of the camp. "Are you working with the contractors to build the new water towers?"

"I am," Toland responded. "But please, don't let me keep you from your exercise. I'm sure Sergeant Agar needs a good run to keep him in shape, too." He waved his hand as if granting her passage.

All in all, Kinsley was irritated by the man's arrogance in stepping in front of her in the first place. And even more convinced Agar was right to growl at the man. She'd learned to trust her dog's judgment of character.

Toland hadn't said or done anything too far out of the ordinary. Even so, Kinsley couldn't put her finger on it, but she wasn't sure she trusted the man. After all, why did a man stop a lone female soldier just to talk? Didn't the contractors get the same briefing as the military personnel?

Don't fraternize. Period.

As soon as she cleared the buildings, she shook off the prickly feeling at the back of her neck and quickened her pace into a slow, steady jog, with Agar easily keeping up at her side.

Running had never been a joy, but she did it to stay in shape for the semiannual fitness test and to be able to keep up with the physical demands of the job. She had to be in shape to walk long miles carrying a heavy rucksack. She might also be required to run into and out of bad situations. She expected Agar to be fit; she required nothing less of herself.

She ran along the track circling the containerized living units, staring at the stark desert beyond. She could glimpse a bit of the blue waters of the Gulf of Aden. No matter how hot, she preferred running outdoors than in the air-conditioned fitness center on the treadmills set up for residents of the camp. If Agar had to run in the heat, then she would do no less. The peace of the desert, with the wind off the water and the salty tang in the air, lulled her into a trance, nearly clearing her thoughts of the man Agar had come close to slamming into earlier.

Kinsley had to admit McGuire had appeal, unlike William Toland, who was perhaps old enough to be her father. Knowing McGuire was a SEAL made her all the more curious about the man. Anyone who had gone through BUD/S training had to be not only physically fit, but also mentally equipped to handle the most extreme environments and situations.

Based on the man's broad shoulders pulling tautly at his uniform, he was fit. But she wasn't sure about his mental fitness. For a long moment, he'd stared at her before actually opening his mouth. Perhaps he'd been hit once too often in the head and had suffered a brain injury.

At least that's what Kinsley told herself. She preferred to come up with reasons she should stay away from the man rather than reasons to fall under his spell. She hadn't joined the army to get married. And fraternization at Camp Lemonnier was strictly forbidden.

Footsteps sounded behind her, disturbing her not-so-peaceful escape.

She tightened her hold on Agar's lead and moved to the outside of the dirt path, making room for the other runner.

Instead of passing her, the runner slowed to match her pace.

She frowned over at him, ready to tell him to move

on, when she noticed it was him…Petty Officer Mc-Guire, the navy SEAL who had been occupying entirely too many of her thoughts since she'd run into him minutes before.

"Mind if I join you?" he asked with a grin.

She shrugged and kept moving. "Can't stop you."

"All you have to say is *shove off*, and I'll leave you alone," he said. "Sometimes it's nice to have a running buddy to fill the time."

"I actually have one," she said, and tipped her head toward Agar.

As if he could understand, Agar glanced up at her, his tongue lolling to the side.

"I see." With a twist of his lips, McGuire gave a curt nod. "Then I'll leave you two to your workout." And he picked up his pace, leaving Kinsley behind.

For a moment, Agar strained at the leash, wanting to keep up with the jogger ahead.

Kinsley gave him a sharp command. "Heel."

The German shepherd immediately fell in step with her, looking up at Kinsley and back to McGuire as if to tell her he could easily catch the man.

"I suppose I was rude," Kinsley admitted to Agar.

Agar looked up at her words, his mouth open, tongue hanging out the side. He appeared to be smiling, when in fact he was only trying to keep cool in the incredible heat.

"It's just as well. He has red hair. I make it a point not to get involved with men while I'm deployed. But even if we weren't deployed, I couldn't date the man.

He has red hair. Our babies would all be doomed to red hair." She shuddered. "I wouldn't wish all of my children to that lot in life. Not if I have a choice."

Her gaze followed the SEAL as he ran to one corner of the huge field, turned and kept running, his powerful thighs pushing him forward with ease.

Kinsley's heart beat faster and her breathing became more labored as she watched the man's tight buttocks and well-defined legs. If she were into gingers, he'd be the one to catch. Thank goodness she wasn't.

Nevertheless, she slowed to a fast walk, letting McGuire widen the gap between them. She didn't want to risk running into him again at the end of her run. The man had *complication* written all over him.

When she arrived back at her quarters, she found a note stuck to the door.

Meeting at command center ASAP.

Kinsley had never received a message like that. Her pulse kicked up a notch, but she focused on staying calm. For all she knew, someone might have lodged a complaint about her exercising Agar too close to the living quarters. Or they were switching her to night shift.

She refused to get excited and dare to think she might be sent on an actual mission.

Chapter Two

T-Mac had just stepped out of the shower facility when Big Jake found him.

"Meeting in the command center, now," Big Jake said.

"Give me two minutes to get dressed." T-Mac hurried in his flip-flops toward his quarters, threw on his uniform, hat and boots and ran out the door, buttoning his jacket as he went. He jogged all the way to the command center and stepped inside the air-conditioned containerized office unit.

Inside, his team sat around a long, narrow table. Navy Commander Trevor Ward stood at the head of the table, his gaze on T-Mac as he entered. "Now that we're all here, let's get this party started."

T-Mac remained standing near the door, his curiosity piqued, his adrenaline pumping. He preferred missions to boredom any day.

"We're all ready to mobilize back to the States—" the commander held up his hand "—and as far as everyone is concerned, we will still be leaving in four days. However, we just received intel on a trade deal going down tonight on the border of Somalia."

The team waited quietly for Commander Ward to continue.

"You might ask what we have to do with trade in this area. But here's the deal. Someone from around here has been funneling shipments of weapons from around Camp Lemonnier to the Al-Shabaab terrorists in Somalia. Intel intercepted a text communication from a burner cell phone nearby. Apparently, there will be handoff of a shipment conducted tonight in one of the abandoned, shelled-out villages on the other side of the border between Djibouti and Somalia." He nodded to his assistant, who clicked the keys on a laptop.

A map of the Horn of Africa blinked up on the whiteboard behind the commander.

Commander Ward turned to point at the location marked with a red dot. "The mission is simple. We go in, capture the traitors involved and return them to camp."

"All in a night's work," Harm said. "What's the catch?"

"Previous attempts by army rangers to recon this village were met with explosives."

"As in mortars and rocket-propelled grenades?" Buck asked.

The commander's lips pressed into a thin line. "Not so easy. IEDs and land mines. That's why we'll have two additional members on our team."

As if on cue, the door behind T-Mac opened and a German shepherd entered, followed by Specialist Kinsley Anderson, still dressed in her PT uniform of shorts, a T-shirt and running shoes.

The woman glanced around the room full of men and lifted her chin. "I'm sorry I'm late. I got here as soon as I received word of the meeting."

"No worries," the commander said. He waved his hand toward her. "Team, meet Specialist Anderson and Sergeant Agar. They will be with us on this mission tonight."

All eyes turned to the only female in the room.

T-Mac's pulse quickened. He'd never been on a mission with a female. Would having a woman in the mix change the dynamics of his team? Not that he was superstitious, but would the others be worried that a woman would jinx their mission?

He glanced around the room at the others' gazes. For the most part, they appeared more curious than apprehensive.

"Anyone have any issues?" the commander asked.

Specialist Anderson's chin rose another notch, her gaze sweeping the room full of men, challenging them with just that one look.

Big Jake shrugged. "I'd be glad to have a dog ahead of us. I've seen what one can do. They're pretty amazing."

"Same," Buck said. "Rather sniff out the bombs than step on one."

The rest of the men voiced agreement.

"Then get ready, you leave in—" Commander Ward glanced down at his watch "—one hour."

T-Mac followed Anderson out of the building. "Do you need help getting ready?" he asked.

"I think I can figure it out," she said, stepping out smartly and moving toward the containerized living quarters.

Falling in step beside her, T-Mac hustled to keep up. "Is this your first mission outside the wire?" he asked.

She tensed and frowned. "I know my job, and I know what to carry and wear into combat. You don't have to coddle me because I'm female."

He held up his hands. "Oh, believe me, I wouldn't dare do that." Then he ruined it with a chuckle. "I'd help out the new guy, male or female. I like to come back with all the people we left with intact."

Her shoulders relaxed. "Sorry. I shouldn't be so defensive."

"I'm sure you have a right to be."

She lifted her shoulders and let them drop. "I get tired of people underestimating my abilities just because I'm a woman."

"I've seen you two in action. I have complete confidence in you and Agar."

The dog lifted his head at the sound of his name and then looked forward again, trotting alongside his handler.

"Well, you don't have to worry about us. We can

handle our job. We'll keep you and your team safe from explosives."

"And we'll do our best to keep you and Agar safe from loose bullets."

She shot him a hint of a smile. "Thanks." By then, they were standing in front of her quarters. Specialist Anderson frowned. "I didn't ask where we should meet."

T-Mac's lips twisted. "We'll be loading up in helicopters. If you like, I can swing by and we can walk over together."

Her frown cleared. "Thanks. I'd appreciate that."

"My pleasure," he said, and left her at her door to hurry toward his own quarters, where he'd gear up for the mission ahead.

In the back of his mind, he couldn't help but worry about the addition to their team. The SEALs trained together. They hadn't trained with a dog handler working out in front of them. Specialist Anderson and Agar might know what they were doing when it came to sniffing out bombs, but they had no experience in hostile environments.

When T-Mac entered the containerized quarters he shared with Harm, his roommate glanced up from assembling his M4A1 rifle with the SOPMOD upgrade. "Hey, T-Mac."

"Harm." T-Mac pulled a hard plastic case out from under his bunk, extracted his rifle and pulled it apart piece by piece. He'd cleaned it after his last mission and had assembled and disassembled it a number of times since. Handling his weapon was second nature.

"Saw you walked the dog handler back to her quarters," Harm said.

"Yeah." T-Mac stiffened. "So?"

Without looking up from what he was doing, Harm continued. "You know we were just kidding about fixing you up with a female, right?"

T-Mac snorted. "No. I fully expect you guys to bombard me with women."

Harm gave a twisted grin. "You're right. But we'd wait until we got back to the States. What with how touchy folks are about not fraternizing while deployed."

With a frown, T-Mac shook his head. "If this is about Specialist Anderson, forget it. I only offered to help her get ready for the mission. She hasn't actually been on one before."

Harm's head shot up. "Never?"

His chest tightening, T-Mac pressed his lips together. "Everyone has to have a first time."

His roommate frowned. "I'd rather it wasn't with us."

"Would you rather she went out with some teenaged infantry soldiers who are barely out of boot camp?"

Harm sighed. "I suppose not. But I don't like the idea of babysitting when we have a mission to accomplish."

T-Mac pulled the bolt from his weapon, inspected

it and shot it back home, reassembling the weapon in record time. "I'd almost rather take my chances with the mines and IEDs than risk losing her and the dog."

"Not me," Harm said. "Remember what happened to Roadrunner when he got too far ahead of the rest of us on that extraction mission in Afghanistan?"

T-Mac's stomach clenched at the memory.

Roadrunner had been point man when he'd stepped on a land mine. Thankfully for Roadrunner, he'd died instantly. The team had been left to pick up the pieces, physically and mentally.

"Hopefully Anderson and Agar know their stuff," T-Mac muttered.

"Yeah. But they're all about sniffing out explosives. We have to worry about the snipers. A lot of money goes into training dogs and handlers."

"And SEALs," T-Mac reminded him.

Harm nodded. "That's a given. I'd like to make it back to the States in four days. Talia will be waiting at my apartment. I let her use it for a place to stay while she's house hunting."

T-Mac shot a glance toward his teammate. "I thought you two were a thing?"

"We are. But I want her to be sure. Moving from Africa back to the States is a big deal. And dating a SEAL won't make it much easier." Harm lifted a shoulder and let it fall. "I don't want to pressure her. She needs time to make up her own mind and be comfortable with herself."

"Before she commits to you?"

"Yeah." Harm grinned. "You know our lives aren't easy even for us. I want her to know how it is and what she can expect before we tie the knot."

"What happened to being confirmed bachelors? I thought we were a team. And now you all have women." T-Mac shook his head. "I don't get it."

Harm chuckled, pulled his steel-plated vest out of his go bag and laid it out on his bunk. "You'll get it when you find the woman who makes you reconsider everything you ever thought to be true."

"Now you're starting to sound sappy. I'm not sure I want to find a woman who makes me go soft." T-Mac strapped a scabbard around his calf and stuck his Ka-Bar knife into it. "Next thing you know, you'll be second-guessing yourself on the battlefield."

"Never." Harm shrugged into his vest and secured several empty magazines into the straps. "Let's quit flapping our gums and go meet up with your cute dog handler."

"She's not *my* dog handler."

"No?" Harm gave him a side-eye glance and raised one eyebrow. "Sure looked like it to the rest of us."

"She's not my dog handler," T-Mac insisted, his tone hard, his lips tight.

"Whatever you say." Harm grabbed his helmet and stepped out of the box. "But between the two of you redheads, you'd make some really cute red-headed babies."

"She's not my redhead," T-Mac said through

clenched teeth as he snagged his helmet and followed Harm. "And we're not having babies."

"Who's having babies?" Buck fell in step behind Harm and T-Mac. "If T-Mac is planning on marrying the dog handler, they can start their own ginger basketball team. Or hockey team. Or whatever team they want. They'd all be gingers."

"We're not getting married. She's not my dog handler, and I'd appreciate it if you wouldn't say anything around her about babies and basketball teams." T-Mac picked up the pace, hoping that by walking faster, his teammates wouldn't have the time nor desire to poke fun at him.

Pitbull and Big Jake stepped out of the quarters they shared.

"What's this about babies and basketball teams?" Pitbull asked. "Is T-Mac marrying his dog handler?"

T-Mac threw his hand in the air. "She's not my dog handler."

Big Jake chuckled. "I think he protests too much. I swear I saw something between the two of them."

"You can't see something that wasn't there." T-Mac sighed. "I get it. This is all part of razzing me because I choose to stay a bachelor and have my pick of women out there while you losers commit to being with one woman for the rest of your lives. I think I have the better deal."

"What deal?" Diesel jogged to catch up to the team. "What did I miss?"

"T-Mac's met his match," Buck said.

T-Mac gritted his teeth. "I didn't."

"His dog handler?" Diesel guessed.

"She's not my dog handler." T-Mac might as well have been talking to a wall.

"Oh, he's going to fall hard," Diesel said. "She's got attitude and a dog. A killer combination. What's not to love about that?"

"I'm not in love. She's not my handler, and I don't even think the dog likes me." He glanced toward the container where Specialist Anderson was staying and debated walking past and letting her find her own way to where the helicopters were parked. But he'd promised to walk with her. He slowed, hoping the rest of the team would walk on without questioning why he was stopping.

But he knew them better than that. They weren't stupid and they would figure it out pretty quickly.

"Look, guys, could you be serious for once?" He turned and raised his hand to knock on the door.

All five of his friends came to a complete stop.

T-Mac groaned as the door opened.

Agar came out first and immediately sniffed T-Mac's crotch.

A rumble of chuckles sounded behind T-Mac.

"I guess the dog likes you after all," Buck muttered.

More chuckles sounded.

Heat rose up T-Mac's neck into his cheeks as he

glanced up at Specialist Anderson. "Don't listen to anything these yahoos say. They're all full of… Well, they're full of it, anyway."

KINSLEY TORE HER gaze away from the SEAL standing in front of her looking all hot and incredibly sexy in his combat gear. Beyond Petty Officer McGuire stood five of the other men who'd been in the command center minutes before. She stepped out of the doorway, looped the strap of her rifle over her shoulder and double-wrapped the dog's lead around her hand. "What am I not supposed to listen to them about?"

"Tell her, T-Mac," one of them encouraged.

"We don't have time for games," McGuire said. "We have a mission to accomplish before we head home."

"You're heading home?" Kinsley asked.

"Four days and a wakeup," the tallest of the group answered.

"Where's home?" Kinsley fell in step with them as they wove their way through the temporary buildings to the landing strip where planes and helicopters parked.

"Little Creek, Virginia," McGuire answered.

"What about you?" one of the guys asked. "Where is your home base?"

"San Antonio, Texas, was my last PCS assignment," Kinsley said.

"That's where they train Military Working Dogs, isn't it?" McGuire asked. "They have a facility at Lackland Air Force Base. Is that where you and Agar received your training?"

She nodded. "I spent the past year in training."

"T-Mac says this is your first assignment since training."

Again, Kinsley nodded. "That's true. Agar was the best in his class. He could find trace amounts of explosives that none of our own detection equipment could pick up." She patted the dog's head. "He's good at what he does. If there are IEDs or land mines, he'll prove himself tonight."

As they reached the helicopters, more SEALs gathered. Ammunition was dispensed. Then it came time for them to load into the helicopters.

Kinsley started for one of the choppers away from McGuire and his group.

The navy commander who'd briefed them caught up to her. "You're riding in the other bird. Stick with T-Mac. He'll make sure you're safe."

"I can take care of myself," Kinsley insisted.

"I understand," the commander said. "But the team isn't used to working with a dog and its handler. It's for their safety as well as yours."

Kinsley couldn't argue with that. Apparently, she was to have a handler. "Yes, sir."

The commander escorted her back to the other helicopter where McGuire, or T-Mac, as his team nick-named him, stood, waiting his turn to climb aboard.

"T-Mac," the commander called out.

The SEAL turned when he saw who was with his superior.

"I have an assignment for you," Commander Ward said.

"Yes, sir," T-Mac replied.

"You're to keep up with Specialist Anderson and Sergeant Agar. Bring them back safely."

T-Mac's eyes narrowed. "Sir?"

Kinsley stiffened.

The SEAL didn't look too excited.

"You heard me," the commander said. "Take care of them out there. You don't know what you'll be up against."

"Yes, sir." T-Mac nodded.

When the others in the helicopter chuckled, T-Mac shot a glare their way.

With the odd feeling she wasn't in on the joke, Kinsley stepped up to the chopper.

"Has Agar been in a helicopter?" T-Mac asked.

Kinsley nodded. "Not only has he been up, he's been hoisted in and out on a cable multiple times. He's calm throughout."

"Good." T-Mac offered her a hand up.

Ignoring the hand, Kinsley motioned for Agar to go first. Then she stepped up into the chopper and found a seat between the tallest guy and one who was stout with a barrel chest. She settled between them and buckled her safety harness, keeping Agar close at her feet.

"I'm Jake," said the tall man. "They call me Big Jake."

Kinsley shook hands with the man. "Nice to meet you, Big Jake."

"I'm Pitbull." The barrel-chested guy stuck out his hand. "Here, you'll need these." He handed her a headset.

She removed her helmet and settled the headset over her ears. Immediately, she could hear static and the pilot and copilot performing a communications check with the passengers.

She watched and listened as each of the SEALs answered, and she committed their names to memory.

"Diesel."

"Pitbull."

"Buck."

"Big Jake."

"Harm."

"T-Mac."

Her heart skipped several beats when T-Mac spoke. He sat in the seat opposite, his gaze on her. When no one else spoke, he winked and touched his finger to his own microphone.

Kinsley realized she'd forgotten to say her name. With heat rising up in her cheeks, she spoke into the mic. "Anderson and Agar."

T-Mac grinned.

A moment later, the helicopter lifted off the ground, swung out over the Gulf of Aden and then turned south, back over the Horn of Africa.

The sun had sunk low on the horizon, bathing the land in a bright orange glow.

If they hadn't been headed into a potentially hostile environment, Kinsley would have enjoyed the view, the sunset and the warm wind blowing in her face. But this was her first real combat assignment. She wasn't scared, but she was anxious to do well.

She sat back in her seat, forcing herself to be calm. Agar needed her full focus. He sensed her every mood and emotion. He needed to know she was in full control of herself as well as him. They'd trained to save lives by finding dangers lurking beneath the surface or behind walls.

For the duration of the flight, she concentrated on reducing her heart rate, breathing deeply and going over everything she'd learned in the intensive training she'd been through with Agar. Dogs weren't deployed unless they were ready. And dog handlers didn't last long in training if they weren't capable, consistent and calm. She'd excelled along with Agar.

All of her training had been for more than inspecting vehicles entering through the post gates.

Agar nudged her foot with his nose and looked up at her.

Kinsley rubbed the dog's snout and scratched him behind his ears.

He laid his head on her lap, as if sensing her unrest.

When Kinsley glanced up again, it was to stare across the darkening fuselage at the SEAL seated across from her. Though she resented feeling like she had to be babysat, she was glad she had someone with more combat experience watching her back.

All too soon, the helicopter touched down. The second one landed beside it.

Kinsley removed the helicopter headset, slipped her helmet on and latched the buckle beneath her chin. She exited the aircraft and stood to the side with Agar while all twelve SEALs alighted, checked their gear and waited for the signal to move out.

T-Mac approached her and handed her a small electronic device. "You'll need these earpieces to hear the team as we move through the village. You'll have to keep them up-to-date while they're looking for our traitor."

Kinsley fitted the device in her ear and spoke. "Testing."

Big Jake took charge, giving directions, performing one last communication check on their radio headsets.

After everyone checked in, Big Jake gathered them in a circle. "The village should be another four clicks to the east. We need to get in, clear the rubble of any enemy combatants and wait for the handoff. Any questions?"

Big Jake nodded toward Kinsley. "Take it, dog soldier."

Kinsley's heartbeat quickened. This was it. She

and Agar had a job to do, lives to save and explosives to find.

She tugged on Agar's lead, sending him in the direction Big Jake indicated. She allowed the dog to run out at the extent of the retractable lead and walked behind him. She carried her rifle in her right hand, the lead in her left.

T-Mac fell in step beside her, his specialized M4A1 at the ready position.

Darkness had settled over the landscape with a blanket of stars lighting their way.

Agar zigzagged back and forth in front of her, his nose to the ground, tail wagging, moving swiftly enough that Kinsley had to hustle to keep up.

One kilometer passed without incident. Then two. As they neared their target, Kinsley slowed Agar, encouraging him to take his time. The team had chosen to approach the abandoned village from the west, establish a defensive position and wait for the party to start. The handoff was supposed to take place at midnight. That gave them a few hours to get in place and hunker down.

From what some of her more experienced counterparts had reported, sometimes it took hours to navigate a quarter-mile stretch. If their adversary considered the location to be worth the effort to defend or sabotage, they could have rigged it with land mines or trip wires hooked to detonators.

Glad for T-Mac's protection, she led the SEALs

toward the crumbled buildings at the edge of the little village.

As they neared the closest of what was left of a mud-and-stick hut, Agar stopped, sniffed and lay down on the ground.

Kinsley's pulse quickened. "He found something."

She marked the spot with a flag and bent to scratch Agar behind the ears, then gave him the command to continue his search. Within a few feet he lay down again.

Marking the new spot, Kinsley worked with Agar, moving a few feet at time, ever closer to the village, at what felt like an excruciatingly slow pace.

"I don't like it," T-Mac said. "If they have a sniper waiting in one of those buildings, they can easily pick us off."

"Unless they figure the explosives will alert them to anyone coming in from this direction," Big Jake said into Kinsley's ear.

She ignored the chatter and continued until she and Agar had identified a clear path to the village through what appeared to be a short field of submerged mines.

Once inside the crumbled walls of the village, Agar moved from structure to structure, sniffing without lying down.

Kinsley didn't let her guard down for a moment. After encountering the mines, she wouldn't put it past whoever set them to have more hidden treasures to keep unwanted visitors out.

She had Agar enter huts along the way, clear them and move on, aiming toward the center of the village and the road that led through the middle.

All the while, T-Mac remained at her side, his weapon ready, hand on the trigger.

As Agar neared the building on the edge of the road, he slowed. His hackles rose on the back of his neck and he uttered a low and dangerous growl.

Kinsley dropped to a squat in the shadow of the nearest building.

T-Mac followed her movement and knelt on one knee at her side. "What's the growl mean?"

"Someone's nearby," Kinsley whispered.

T-Mac held up a hand where the others could see his command to stop.

Kinsley didn't dare look back. All her focus was on Agar and what was in front of the dog.

"We'll take it from here." T-Mac rose and started forward.

Kinsley caught his arm before he could move past her. "But what if there are more explosives?"

"You're not going any farther." T-Mac glanced down at her. "Bring Agar back."

Kinsley didn't like being relegated to the rear. She'd come this far; she wanted to complete her work.

Before she could bring Agar back, the dog turned and entered a building, his growls increasing in volume and intensity.

Kinsley hurried after him.

"Wait," T-Mac called after her.

She had to know Agar was all right. As she ran forward, she pulled her flashlight from her pocket. When she turned into the doorway of the building, she flipped on the switch and shone the light, filtered with a red lens, into the room.

Agar stood with his feet planted and his lips pulled back in a wicked snarl.

As she panned the light around to see what Agar was growling at, a man's face appeared in the glow... a face she knew.

Kinsley gasped but didn't have time to react when the man lifted his rifle and fired point-blank into her chest.

The bullet hit with enough force to knock her backward through the door. She landed flat on her back and lay stunned.

Before she could catch her breath, the world erupted in gunfire around her.

Agar flew out of the building and landed on his side.

"No!" Kinsley screamed silently, though nothing would come from her lungs. She rolled to her side and tried to rise.

Agar yelped, the kind of sound only emitted when an animal was hurt.

Pushing past her own breathlessness and the pain in her chest, Kinsley crawled toward the dog, her heart in her throat, her need to reach Agar foremost in her mind.

Then an explosion went off in the building in

front of her, shooting mud, rock and shrapnel in all directions.

Kinsley felt the force of the blast against her eardrums. Her body was peppered with rock and shrapnel like so many pellets from a shotgun shell. Dust billowed outward, choking the air, blinding Kinsley before she could reach Agar.

A sharp pain ripped through her side; still she staggered to her feet, crying out, "Agar!"

A high-pitched whistling sound screamed through the air.

"Incoming!" T-Mac yelled. Then he hit her from behind, sending her flying through the air to land hard on the packed dirt.

T-Mac landed on top of her, knocking the air from her lungs yet again. At the same time, another explosion rocked the ground she lay against.

Her ears rang, and for a moment she couldn't breathe or move. Dust and debris rained down on them. A darkness so deep closed in on her, threatening to pull her under.

"Agar." She reached out her hand, patting the ground, unable to move or crawl forward. Then her fingers touched fur. A sob rose in her throat as her vision faded and the ringing in her ears became a roar. She couldn't pass out. Agar needed her.

The next thing she knew, she was being lifted into the air. She struggled to get free. "No."

"Be still, Kinsley." T-Mac's voice sounded in her ear. "I'll get you out of here."

"No," she croaked, choking on dust. "Can't leave—"

Gunfire sounded all around.

"I have to get you out of here," T-Mac insisted. "You've been hit."

"Can't leave." She fought him, pounding her fists against his chest.

Big Jake appeared beside her. "Get her out of here."

T-Mac fought to retain his hold on her. "She refuses to go."

"Agar." Kinsley pushed against T-Mac's chest.

"He was hit," T-Mac said.

She swung her legs out of T-Mac's grasp and dropped to the ground. "Not leaving without him." Her knees buckled and she would have crumpled into a heap if T-Mac hadn't been holding on to her.

Again he scooped her up into his arms. "You can't stay here."

"I'll get the dog." Big Jake ran into the swirling dust and reappeared a moment later, carrying Agar.

"Oh, God," Kinsley sobbed. "Agar." Tears streamed from her eyes. "Let me help him."

"Not until we're out of here." T-Mac ran through the village, back the way they'd come. He passed his team as they moved in the opposite direction.

Over T-Mac's shoulder, Kinsley watched for Big Jake. The big man appeared out of the cloud of dust, still holding Agar.

Then, as they cleared the edge of the village, Big Jake staggered and fell to his knees, his arms hitting the ground first, cushioning Agar's landing.

"Stop!" Kinsley screamed. "Big Jake's down."

"I can't stop," T-Mac said. "I can only carry one person at a time."

Behind Big Jake, another one of the SEALs appeared, looped Big Jake's arm over his shoulder and half carried the big man down the path between the flags Kinsley had planted to identify the buried land mines.

Agar remained on the ground…left behind.

"Let me down," Kinsley begged. "Please." She didn't dare struggle, afraid that if she did, she'd make T-Mac stumble and veer into one of the mines. Her strength waned, and a warm wet stickiness spread across her right arm and leg.

"Please, you can't leave Agar. He's my partner. He trusted me." Her voice faded to a whisper as tears trickled down her face and darkness threatened to block out the stars shining above.

The crackle of gunfire and the boom of explosions seemed to be coming from farther and farther away.

Kinsley must have passed out. When she came to, T-Mac was laying her on the floor of a helicopter. When she tried to sit up, her body refused to cooperate. All she could lift was her head, and only for a moment before it dropped to the hard metal floor. "Agar," she said on a sigh.

"Buck, do what you can," T-Mac said. "She's bleeding in several places."

"Don't worry about me," she said. "Please, go find Agar."

No one seemed to be listening as they pulled off her helmet, unbuckled her protective vest and applied pressure to her wounds.

"Shh, you're going to be all right." T-Mac leaned over her, brushing her hair from her face, while someone else ripped her uniform jacket away from her leg.

The rumble of rotor blades sounded and the helicopter lifted from the ground.

As they rose into the air, Kinsley reached out a hand. "Agar."

T-Mac took her hand. "We'll take care of you."

"But who will take care of Agar?" she whispered.

And then the sounds of the rotor blades faded, and the world went black.

Chapter Three

T-Mac stayed with Specialist Anderson from the moment he carried her out of the village until they wheeled her into the medical facility at Camp Lemonnier. At that point, the medical team on standby grabbed him and made him take a gurney as well.

"You're bleeding," one of the medics said.

"I don't care. I promised to take care of Anderson." He pushed to his feet and slipped in something wet on the floor.

The medic grabbed his arm and steadied him. "She's in good hands. And you can't go back with her."

"But it was my responsibility to take care of her." And he'd failed. Miserably.

The physician on call appeared in front of T-Mac, a frown furrowing his brow. "You might not care about your own injuries, but you're putting everyone else in this facility in danger with the amount of blood you're getting on the floor. Take a seat, SEAL."

At the command in the doctor's voice, T-Mac sat on the gurney.

The medics stripped him of his body armor and uniform jacket and cut away the leg of his trousers.

In minutes the doctor had fished out the shrapnel, stitched the wound and applied a bandage.

The medics cleaned up the blood from the floor and set his gear on a chair beside the examination table.

T-Mac pushed to a sitting position and reached for his boots. Once he had his feet in them, he slid off the table to stand on the floor. He swayed slightly.

The medic was there, helping him stay upright. "Hey, you're going to rip a stitch if you're not careful."

"I want to see Specialist Anderson."

"They're taking care of her now." The young medic, who couldn't be more than nineteen years old, released his arm. "I'll go check on her and let you know how it's going." He helped him out of the room and nodded toward the front of the building. "In the meantime, you can take a seat in the lobby. I'll bring your gear."

Gritting his teeth, T-Mac turned away as another gurney entered the building with Big Jake on it.

His face was pale, but his eyes were open. He grabbed T-Mac's arm as he passed. "How's the dog soldier?"

"They're working on her now." T-Mac scanned his friend. "Where were you hit?"

"Took a bullet in the buttocks." Big Jake laughed

and grimaced. "Only hurts when I laugh, or move, or hell, anything. I'll be glad when they get it out."

T-Mac stood back, his gaze going to the medics pushing the gurney. "Take care of my friend."

"We've got this. You might want to take a seat while you're waiting," the medic who'd helped him said. "You lost a little bit of blood yourself."

T-Mac made his way to the lobby. The window looking out was still dark.

As promised, the medic delivered his gear, setting it on the floor beside a chair.

Wearing his torn pants, the air-conditioned air cool on his exposed leg, T-Mac paced the short distance between chairs. He prayed the female dog handler and Big Jake would be all right. Part of him wanted to be back in the bombed-out village, wreaking havoc on those who'd hurt his team.

Seeing Anderson blown back out of the building by the power of a point-blank attack made his gut clench. He'd tried to grab her arm before she went in, but she'd been too fast, worried about her dog. He should have known she'd do something like that and thought ahead. She was his responsibility. Even if the commander hadn't tagged him with the job, he would have taken it anyway.

As he stared at his body armor and helmet, he wondered if the rest of his team was still fighting or if they'd brought the little village under control.

The whole mission had felt as if it had been a fiasco from the very beginning…as if they had been led into the chute like lambs to slaughter.

Unfortunately, Specialist Anderson had been first up. She'd taken a bullet to her armor-plated chest. Thankfully, she'd worn her protective gear, or she'd be dead. As it was, the mortar having landed near them had taken its toll. If she didn't die of a punctured or collapsed lung from the blunt force of being fired on at close range, she might die from the multiple shrapnel wounds across her arms and legs. Or suffer from traumatic brain injury.

He didn't feel the stitches pinching since the doctor had given him a local anesthetic, but he felt ridiculous in his one-legged pants.

All the while he sat in the lobby, his teammates could be facing the fight of their lives, and he wasn't there to help.

An hour passed, and the medic came out. "Your friend, Petty Officer Schuler, is going to be okay. He should be out shortly."

Minutes later, Big Jake limped out into the lobby, wearing what T-Mac assumed were borrowed gym shorts and his T-shirt.

A medic carried his body armor and helmet, as well as his shirt and the remainder of his pants. "I can help you get back to your quarters when the shift changes in an hour," he promised. He glanced over his shoulder. "I have to get back in there."

"Wait." T-Mac took a step forward. "What's the status of Specialist Anderson?"

The medic shook his head. "They removed all the shrapnel, but she's still unconscious. They were waiting to see if she'd come out of it on her own, but she got kind of combative, so they sedated her. The doctor thinks she might have a concussion. We've called for transport to get her to the next level of care. They'll either take her to Ramstein in Germany or back to the States."

T-Mac's chest tightened. "How soon?"

"As soon as we can scramble a crew and medical staff to fly out on a C-130." The medic turned. "Now, if you'll excuse me, I need to get back." He disappeared before T-Mac could ask any more questions.

Big Jake laid a hand on T-Mac's shoulder. "I'm sorry about your dog handler."

For every time T-Mac had corrected his teammates, he knew he'd been lying to himself. He didn't know Kinsley Anderson well, nor did he have any ties to her, other than having been assigned to protect her. Still, he had felt she was his dog handler and that he was responsible for seeing to her safety.

The door to the medical facility burst open behind T-Mac and Big Jake. Buck, Harm, Diesel and Pitbull pushed through, covered in dust and smelling of gunpowder.

"Thank God you're both okay." Buck clapped a hand to T-Mac's back.

"We didn't know what had happened to you when you took off," Pitbull said.

Diesel nodded toward their pant legs and grinned.

"New fashion statement in uniform trousers?" Then his smile faded. "You're okay?"

Big Jake snorted. "Other than a stitch here and there, we'll survive."

"What about T-Mac's dog handler?" Harm asked.

T-Mac's jaw tightened. "They're going to ship her out to the next level of medical support." He turned to Harm. "What about Agar? What happened to the dog?" T-Mac knew the first thing Kinsley would want to know was if her dog made it out alive.

Harm shook his head. "We got him onto the helicopter and carried him to the camp veterinarian. I can't tell you whether he'll make it. He was nonresponsive when we delivered him, but I think he still had a heartbeat."

When Kinsley recovered enough to ask, she'd receive yet another blow if the dog didn't make it. T-Mac wanted to know more about Agar's condition, but he wasn't leaving the medical facility until the army specialist did.

"You might as well get some rest," Big Jake said. "You can't do anything for her now."

"I know. But I'm staying," he said.

Big Jake nodded. "You know it wasn't your fault she was hurt."

T-Mac's fists knotted, but he didn't say anything.

Big Jake touched his arm. "You couldn't have known the dog would dart into that building, or that someone was there waiting to shoot her."

"That's right," Buck stated. "She's lucky she had on her body armor, or she wouldn't be alive—"

Pitbull elbowed Buck in the ribs. "She's going to be okay. The docs will take good care of her. And when they get her to a real hospital, they'll make sure she gets even better care."

T-Mac knew all that, but he wouldn't feel better about any of it until he saw the dog handler standing in front of him, giving him attitude.

"If you two are up to it, the CO wants a debrief," Harm said. "He's out for blood. The way we see it, we were set up, plain and simple."

"Did you find the guy who shot Specialist Anderson?" T-Mac asked.

Harm's lips thinned. "We thought we'd find pieces of him after the explosion, but he got away. There was a back door to that hut."

Anger seared through T-Mac's veins. "He got away?"

"Yeah," Buck said. "And the only guy they left behind was in no condition to give us any answers."

"He was dead," Pitbull said.

"Shot in the back," Diesel finished.

"Not only were they waiting for us," Harm said, "but they had their escape plan in place before we got there."

Buck's eyes narrowed. "Someone tipped them off about what time we left. We got there well before the arranged trade deadline."

"Any others hurt besides the three of us and Agar?" T-Mac asked.

"No," Pitbull said. "When the dust settled, they were gone in a couple of pickup trucks. We would have gone after them, but we figured the dog needed medical attention."

"What exactly happened to the dog handler?" Harm wanted to know.

"She was shot in the chest by whomever was in that hut."

"That'll give her nightmares." Diesel shook his head. "Seeing the face of the man who shot you would leave an indelible image in your mind."

T-Mac snorted. "She was more concerned about Agar being hurt than the fact she'd nearly been killed."

"I hope they make it." Big Jake gently rubbed a hand over his backside. "The whole mission was a disaster."

T-Mac ran a hand through his hair. "Absolutely. Tell the commander what I told you. I'll be here, if he wants to hear it from me in person."

"Will do." Big Jake limped out of the facility with the others on their way to the debrief.

T-Mac paced the lobby again, his frustration growing with each step. He hoped he could be around when Kinsley came to. He wanted to let her know how sorry he was for not keeping her and Agar safe.

Just when T-Mac was ready to ignore the rules and march back to Kinsley's bed, the medic returned.

"She's still out of it," he said. "But you can come back and sit with her."

KINSLEY HOVERED BETWEEN the dark and the light. Every time she felt as if she were surfacing from a deep, black well, she stretched out her hand only to slip back into it. No matter how hard she climbed and scraped her hands on the hard stone walls, she couldn't seem to get to the top. Her fingers grew chilled from the coldness of the stones.

And then warmth wrapped around her hand.

She quit fighting to climb and lay back, basking in the warmth radiating from her hand up her arm and throughout her body.

A deep voice came to her through the black abyss.

"Kinsley, wake up and tell me I'm wrong."

That voice made her want to wake, but that well she'd been clawing her way out of wouldn't let her go.

"Kinsley, you're going to be okay. You just need to wake up and give me all kinds of grief for not taking care of you."

Who was talking to her? And what was he talking about? She tried to open her eyes but she didn't have the strength. So, she lay listening to the warm, deep tones, letting them wash over her, fill her, hold her up when she couldn't stay afloat in the bottomless well. The voice permeated her insides while a strong hand cupped hers, providing heat when she felt so very cold.

Images and sensations swirled in an endless cyclone, refusing to coalesce into anything she could recognize. Faces, dust, fur, sounds, blinding flashes, all spinning inside, making her dizzy, forcing her back into that well, away from the light.

"Kinsley, sweetheart, you're going to be all right. Open your eyes. You'll see. I should have been the one entering that building. You and Agar wouldn't have been hurt if I'd gone first. You have to be okay. Agar is going to need you."

Agar? The word was odd, yet familiar. Still, she couldn't remember why. Nothing made sense. The only anchor keeping her from drowning in the whirlpool threatening to take her under was the voice in the darkness urging her toward the light.

As the black abyss pulled her under, she tightened her hold on the big hand.

MINUTES, HOURS or days later—Kinsley couldn't tell—she blinked her eyes open and stared at the top of an auburn head lying on the sheet beside her. She wasn't in her apartment back in San Antonio. Then she remembered—she'd deployed. Her brow furrowed. To where? She thought hard, the truth just out of her grasp.

She was in the army. They'd sent her on a long flight to…

Nothing.

Frustration made her want to hit something. But when she tried to clench her fist, she couldn't. Someone was holding her hand.

Again, she stared at the head on the sheet beside her. Perhaps the man who owned the head was also the one holding her hand.

But why?

The astringent scent of disinfectant assailed her nostrils. Her gaze moved from the stranger's head to the walls around her. Once again, she realized she wasn't in an apartment, and based on the unusual bed, the bright overhead lights and the monitor tracking her heartbeat, she had to be in some kind of hospital.

Had she been hurt? Kinsley took inventory of her body. Twinges of pain answered for her. Stinging on the surface of her arms and legs let her know she had cuts and abrasions. Her chest felt bruised, and breathing deeply made it slightly worse.

But who was the man with his head on her bed? And what was she forgetting that was so important? Something tugged at her mind, something she should remember, but couldn't.

"Psst," she said.

The man remained facedown on the sheet.

"Hey." When she spoke, her voice sounded like a frog's croak.

The head stirred and lifted. Blue eyes opened, and ginger brows knitted together. "Kinsley?" the man said.

"Yes, that's me." She frowned. "But who are you?"

He sat up straight in the chair beside her bed and pushed a hand through his hair. "I'm T-Mac. Don't you remember me?"

Her frown deepened, making her head hurt. "If I remembered, would I be asking?"

He chuckled. "You still have your bite. We met yesterday, near your quarters."

"Quarters?" She looked around. "These aren't my quarters."

His brows pinched together again. "No. You're in the Djibouti medical facility."

"Why am I here?" she asked.

"You were injured in a skirmish in Somalia."

"Skirmish?" she asked, feeling like she was missing a chunk of her memory. And it was scaring her. "What day is it?"

He told her the date. "You were shot and involved in an explosion."

She gasped, her heartbeat fluttering uncontrollably. "What was I doing in Somalia?" The green line on the monitor jumped erratically.

The auburn-haired man pushed to his feet. "Let me get the doctor."

"I'm okay," she said. "I'm okay," she repeated, as if to remind herself. "I just can't remember any of that."

He didn't listen, leaving the room in a hurry.

Kinsley lifted her head. A sharp pain slashed

through her forehead. She lay back, closed her eyes and let it abate before she opened her eyes again.

By then T-Mac had returned with a man in a white coat. He introduced himself as her doctor. She couldn't commit his name to her memory with the pain throbbing in her head.

He shone a light into her eyes. "Do you remember what happened to you?"

She tried to shake her head, remembering too late that it caused pain. Kinsley winced. "No." Her heart beat fast and her hands shook as she pressed her fingertips to her temple. "I can't remember what day it is."

"Do you know who the president of the United States is?" the doctor asked.

She thought, but couldn't come up with a name. "No."

"What about where you were born?" he persisted.

The more she tried to remember, the worse her head hurt. "I can't remember." A tear slipped from the corner of her eye to run down her cheek.

The doctor patted her hand. "Don't be too alarmed. You had a concussion. Temporary memory loss can be a side effect."

"Will it come back?" Kinsley asked. "Will I remember where I'm from and who the president is?"

He smiled down at her. "You should. Give yourself time to recover. We're trying to get a transport to send you back to a higher-level medical-care facility, but we can't seem to find a C-130 we can tap into for the next couple days. You might be stuck with us."

"I'm fine," she said, and pushed up on her elbows. "I need to get back to work." She shook her head. "If only I could remember what work I do."

The doctor touched her shoulder. "Don't strain your brain. The memories will return, given time."

She lay back on the bed, her gaze following the doctor as he left her room. Kinsley wanted to call him back, to make him give her some pill or potion to force her memories to return. Not knowing things was confusing and frightening.

Her gaze shifted to T-Mac. "Why are you here?"

He smiled. "I wanted to make sure you were going to be okay."

"I'm okay. You don't have to be here. I'm sure you have more important things to do."

"Do you mind if I stay? I'm not on duty or anything. After being here all night, I feel invested in your well-being."

She shrugged. "Suit yourself. I'm probably going to go back to sleep. Maybe when I wake up again, I'll remember what I've forgotten." She laughed, the sound catching on a sob. "I don't even know what I've forgotten."

He lifted her hand and gave it a light squeeze. "I'd fill you in, but I barely know you."

"Then you're no help." She closed her eyes but didn't try to pull her hand free. Holding on to T-Mac was the lifeline she needed at that moment. If that made her weak…so be it. Until she got her memories back, she felt as though she'd been set adrift on an ocean, far from shore.

"What exactly happened?" she asked.

His eyes narrowed as if he were assessing her.

She waved her free hand. "I'm a soldier. Don't pull your punches. Give it to me." Then her eyes widened and a smile lifted her lips. "I'm a soldier."

T-Mac smiled. "See? Your memory's already coming back." He nodded. "We entered a village with the intention of getting there ahead of people coming to make a weapons handoff. We ran into resistance. You were shot in the chest. The team was overwhelmed by incoming grenades and mortars, and we backed out to regroup. Fortunately, you were wearing body armor, or the outcome could have been very different."

"That's it?" She studied T-Mac. He wasn't telling her everything. "What else?"

"Agar was injured."

That name. She should know that name. She didn't want to say it, but she couldn't remember who Agar was.

T-Mac's gaze pinned hers, his lips pressing together for a moment. "Your dog."

As if a floodgate had been unleashed, images and memories poured over Kinsley, all revolving around Agar, his training, her training as a dog handler and the heat of summer in San Antonio, Texas. She tried to breathe, but her lungs were constricted, the air refusing to enter or leave. "Agar," she mouthed. Her hand squeezed his tightly.

"He's with the veterinarian. I haven't been there yet to check his status."

Kinsley pushed to a sitting position. Her head spun and pain knifed through her temple. "Have to see him."

T-Mac pressed a hand to her shoulder. "You're not going anywhere until the doc clears you to move."

"I'm going." She shoved his hand away and swung her legs over the side of the bed. That's when she noticed she was only wearing a hospital gown and not much else. "Where are my clothes?"

"They cut away the trousers and shirt to get to your shrapnel wounds."

"Great. I don't suppose I can walk across the camp in this gown?" She glanced down at the flimsy hospital dress and back up at T-Mac.

"I'll bring a change of clothes for you."

"Thanks." Her brows rose.

"Oh, you mean now?" He grinned. "I should say, I'll get your clothing when the doctor releases you to go back to your quarters."

"I'm leaving." She scooted her bottom to the edge of the mattress. "With or without clothes."

"Specialist Anderson, you haven't been released from my care." The doctor chose that moment to return to her room. "Until that time, you're under my command. You leave, and I'll have to report you as AWOL."

Kinsley frowned. "I need to see my dog."

"You can see your dog when I release you. I want to keep you one more night. If everything looks good in the morning, I'll sign your release orders." The doctor shone his penlight into her eyes, listened to her heartbeat and then left her alone again with T-Mac.

"I'll check on Agar and let you know how he's doing," T-Mac said.

Kinsley wanted to see for herself, but she couldn't risk her career by disobeying orders. "Okay. But could you go now?"

T-Mac chuckled, the rich tone warming her in the air-conditioned room. "Going." He performed an about-face and marched to the door, where he turned back. "Don't go anywhere. I'll be back in a few minutes."

"You might want to shower before you return." She wrinkled her nose. "You smell."

He leaned close and inhaled. "You're no bed of roses either, Specialist." He moved out of range of her swinging arm and winked.

She watched him leave in his torn pants and dirty uniform jacket. Even with dried blood smeared across his leg, he was handsome.

Kinsley crossed her arms over her chest, every nerve in her body urging her to jump out of bed and race after him, to go to the vet's office. Agar had to be okay. He was more than just a working dog to her. He was her only friend.

The image of T-Mac's head lying on the bed beside

her returned. He'd been by her side throughout the night when he didn't have to be. Why had he stayed for a relative stranger?

Now that T-Mac was gone, Kinsley felt alone and overwhelmed. At least she had part of her memory back.

Agar. She could remember every detail of her dog and the training they'd gone through to make him the best explosives-sniffing dog he could be.

But no amount of training made either one of them bulletproof.

Kinsley prayed Agar would be okay. And she hoped T-Mac would hurry back. Not only for news on her dog, but because she already missed holding his hand.

Chapter Four

T-Mac hurried to his quarters and grabbed a clean uniform and his shaving kit. After a quick trip to the shower unit, he felt almost human. His leg stung where his stitches were, but he'd get over it soon enough. The injury wouldn't keep him from a mission, and it sure as hell wouldn't keep him from checking on Kinsley.

On his way back to the medical facility, he swung through the chow hall and snagged a couple of sandwiches and pieces of lemon pound cake. He had them wrapped in cellophane and tucked them in the large pockets of his jacket.

Next stop was the camp veterinarian. When he entered, he found Harm talking to the vet with Agar sitting at his feet.

"It's the darnedest thing," the vet was saying. "One minute he was unconscious, the next he was up and moving around as if nothing had happened. I watched him through the night, but he seems to have suffered no lasting damage from the explosion." The vet handed over the lead to Harm. "He's been fed and has had plenty of water for now. You might test his abilities before he returns to duty. And he could use some exercise. He's been cooped up in a crate until now."

"Will do," Harm said, and handed the lead to T-Mac. "I'm sure your dog handler would like to see her dog."

T-Mac grinned. "I'm sure she would." He reached down to scratch Agar behind the ears. "I'll take him out for a run first." He nodded toward the vet. "Thanks."

"My pleasure. He's a well-behaved animal."

He had to be. Military Working Dogs were selected based on physical ability, temperament and intelligence. Agar had all that going for him, plus a rigorous training program of which Specialist Anderson had been a major part.

T-Mac and Agar followed Harm out of the veterinarian's building.

Harm stopped and faced T-Mac. "How's your dog handler?"

T-Mac smiled. "She's awake and talking." His smile faded.

Harm's brow creased. "But?"

"She's suffering some temporary amnesia."

"Not good."

"No kidding. The doctor thinks she'll get most of her memory back."

"Do you think she saw the man who shot her?"

He shrugged. "It was dark. Even if she did see him, there's no guarantee she'll remember."

"That's too bad."

"It's too bad he got away." T-Mac clenched his fists. That man had fired with all intentions of killing Kinsley. She would be dead had her body armor not protected her.

"The CO wants to see you when you get a chance." Harm held up his hand. "He was satisfied with what we told him, so he said no hurry."

"Good." He wanted to get back to Kinsley as soon as he exercised Agar. "I'll stop by later, after she goes to sleep."

"I'll let him know."

"Did he say anything about the mission?"

"He was hot." Harm bent to smooth his hand over Agar's head and then glanced up at T-Mac. "Someone around here tipped off our quarry. They were ready for us."

"The only people who knew where we were going were our team and the helicopter pilots."

"The commander has the intel folks interviewing the crews and maintenance people," Harm said. "I'll let you know if they learn anything."

"Thanks." T-Mac glanced toward the containerized living units. "Big Jake doing okay?"

"He's sore, but he'll live. The commander wanted him to sit out the next mission, but Big Jake laughed and told him he might as well go. Sitting wasn't an option."

T-Mac chuckled.

"What about you?" Harm pointed to his leg.

"Just a flesh wound. I'm in if they go after the people who did this to us."

"We're all in. You think your dog handler will join us?"

"God, I hope not." He hated to think of Kinsley back in the line of fire. She might not be so lucky next time. "The doc said they're trying to get a transport to carry her to the next level of care. But now that she's awake and coherent, they might change their minds."

"Awake and coherent is a good sign," Harm said. "I can see you're anxious to get back to her. Don't let me hold you up."

"Thanks for checking on Agar." T-Mac left Harm and half walked, half jogged around the camp, giving Agar the exercise he needed. From what he could tell, the dog had completely recovered. At one point, while they were passing the motor pool, Agar growled low in his chest.

With a quick glance around, T-Mac couldn't identify what set off the dog. He'd seen Agar's behavior when he found explosives. He hadn't growled, just lain down beside the find. The only other time he'd seen the dog growl had been before he'd gone into the building with the rebel who'd shot Kinsley.

After he'd walked Agar for fifteen minutes, he headed for the medical facility and strolled through the door as if he owned the place. Bravado might get him past the guy manning the front desk.

"Excuse me," a voice called out behind T-Mac.

He slowed, pulling Agar up on a short leash. "Yes?"

"I'm pretty sure animals aren't allowed in the facility." The young man stood.

"This isn't just an animal. This is Sergeant Agar. He outranks you. You might show him a little more respect."

"You're kidding, right?" The young man's brow twisted.

"Sergeant Agar is on his way to see his handler, Specialist Anderson."

"Oh." The young man sat back in his seat, a worried frown still pulling at his brow. "I guess that's okay, then."

"Right." T-Mac marched past him to the room where he'd left Kinsley. When he entered, he did a double take. The bed was empty. He walked back out and went to the next room only to turn around and come back.

Agar tugged at his lead.

T-Mac released him and he ran for the door to the adjoining bathroom and sniffed at the gap beneath.

The door opened and Kinsley stepped out, holding the back of her gown together behind her. When she saw Agar, she let go and dropped to her knees to hug the German shepherd.

He nuzzled her, licked her face and wagged his tail.

"Thank God you're okay," she whispered, tears

running down her face. She ran her hands over his body and legs. "Did you get hurt?" She checked him over thoroughly, blinking back her tears. When she was done, she looked up at T-Mac. "Thank you for bringing him."

T-Mac smiled. "I think he missed you."

"Even if he didn't, I missed him." She hugged the dog's neck.

A twinge of envy rippled through T-Mac. He found himself wishing he was the dog, being lavished with all the attention and hugs. But the smile on Kinsley's face made T-Mac's day brighter. "Now that you have Agar, I suppose you don't need me anymore."

Her eyes widened and she straightened. "You can stay, if you like. Though it's horribly boring being stuck in bed all day. I don't know why the doctor doesn't let me go. I feel fine. And Agar needs to be exercised. I have to know, the next time we're out, that he'll be able to sniff out explosives."

"I walked him before we came into the facility. And tomorrow should be soon enough to test his skills," T-Mac assured her. "In the meantime, do you want me to take him back to my quarters?"

Her eyes widened and her hold on Agar tightened. "He sleeps in my room, with me."

He leaned close and dropped his voice to a whisper. "I bet if Agar's really quiet no one will notice if he stays."

Kinsley pushed to her feet and walked to the bed.

Agar followed, his body pressed against her legs.

Kinsley slipped beneath the sheets and lay back.

Agar paced around the bed, lifting his nose to sniff at Kinsley. Then he leaped up onto the foot of the bed.

Kinsley laughed and moved over.

Agar stretched out beside her and rested his snout on her arm.

The image of the two of them lying against the white sheets made T-Mac's heart swell. For a fleeting moment, he wished he was Agar, and that he'd put that happy smile on Kinsley's face.

She closed her eyes and sighed. "I guess I can stay another night as long as Agar's with me."

T-Mac cleared his throat. "Since you don't need me, I'll go."

Kinsley's eyes flew open. "Do you have to?"

He shrugged. "No. My buddies are covering for me with my commander."

She held out her hand. "I think they gave me a sedative. Could you stay until I go to sleep?" Her lips twisted. "You don't have to if you don't want to."

He chuckled. "Playing second fiddle to a dog isn't quite a compliment, but I'll take it."

T-Mac pulled the chair close and gathered her hand in his, reveling at how small it was in his, yet how strong and supple her fingers were.

Agar leaned his long snout over Kinsley's body, sniffed T-Mac's hand once and then laid his head back on Kinsley's other side, seemingly satisfied T-Mac wouldn't harm the dog handler.

For a long moment, she said nothing. T-Mac assumed she was sleeping.

"Don't tell anyone," Kinsley whispered, her eyes closed, her breathing slow and steady.

T-Mac stroked the back of her hand. "Tell anyone what?"

"That the tough-as-nails army soldier needed to hold a navy SEAL's hand."

"I could find another poor soul to hold your hand, if you like." His fingers tightened around hers. "Maybe even an army puke," he offered, but he really didn't want to relinquish his hold.

"No need to disturb anyone else." She lay for a while with her eyes closed.

T-Mac studied her face. Freshly washed, free of any makeup, she had that girl-next-door appeal, with a sprinkling of freckles across her nose and cheeks.

T-Mac had the sudden urge to kiss those freckles.

"Why did you want to be a SEAL?" Kinsley's voice yanked T-Mac back to reality.

He barely knew this woman. They were deployed. Fraternization could get them both kicked out of the military, or hit with an Article 15, which would put a black mark on their records and keep them from getting promoted.

"I joined the navy because I didn't want to be a farmer," he said. "My father owns a farm in Nebraska. I grew up running tractors and combines through the summer. He inherited the farm from his father, who inherited it from his father."

"Was your father disappointed when you didn't want to take over the farm?"

T-Mac shrugged. "Not really. I think when he was a teenager, he had dreams of traveling the world and doing something else with his life. But his father had a heart attack and he stayed to take care of the crops and his mother. And he never left."

"Any siblings?" she asked.

"A younger sister." He grinned. "And she's all about the farming. She's in college now, studying agriculture and researching all kinds of things that will help improve crops and yield. My father is so proud of her."

"And he's not proud of you?" Kinsley asked.

T-Mac nodded. "He is. I'm doing what he would have wanted to do. Whenever I can, I send pictures of some of the places I've been. I think he lives vicariously through me. One of these days, I hope to take him and my mother to Europe on vacation. I want them to see Italy, Greece, Spain and France. My father is a big history buff. He'd love it."

Kinsley smiled, her eyes open, the green color seeming deeper. "Sounds like you had a good childhood. You must love your folks a lot."

He nodded. "I miss them, but I also love what I'm doing." T-Mac tilted his head. "What about you? What made you join the army?"

Her lips twisted. "I didn't feel like I had a lot of choices. My mother didn't have the money to send me to college. I joined the army to build a better life for myself. When I get out, I plan on going to college."

"What do you want to study?"

"I don't know yet. I might go into nursing. But for now, I love working with the dogs. Agar in particular."

As if he knew she was talking about him, Agar rested his head over her belly.

Kinsley stroked the dog's neck. "Working with Agar has taught me more about life and living than all twenty-something years of my life."

"How so?"

"I grew up with a single mother. She worked two jobs to keep a roof over my head and food on the table. I didn't see her enough."

"Sounds like you were pretty much on your own."

"I was, from about ten on. I didn't have many close friends in school because I didn't join any extracurricular activities. I couldn't. I had to ride the bus home. Walking wasn't an option. Between home and high school were some pretty sketchy neighborhoods. So I went home on the bus and locked the doors. I guess you could say I was pretty introverted. Handling Agar taught me patience with others and helped bring me out of my shell."

"How did you get in with the dogs?" T-Mac asked.

"I was working on a detail near the canine unit at Fort Hood, Texas. I asked how I could get into the program. My first sergeant helped me apply, and here I am." She laughed. "My first real mission and I blew it."

"You didn't blow it." T-Mac squeezed her hand. "Someone tried to blow you away."

She touched a hand to her chest. "Feels like it."

"Bruised?"

"Just sore." Her eyebrows dipped. "But not too sore I can't go back to work."

"I'm sure you let the doctor know."

"Damn right I did." Her chin tilted upward. "Agar and I have work to do...lives to save."

"Yes, you do." Though he didn't like the idea of Kinsley and Agar going out on point again. "About last night... Did you see the face of the man who shot you?"

Kinsley closed her eyes and scrunched her face. After a minute, she shook her head. "I can't remember even going out with the team. How did we get where we were going?"

T-Mac shook his head. "By helicopter."

Her eyes narrowed. "That's right. You walked me to the helicopter pad."

"Just me?" he prompted.

Kinsley sighed. "That's all I remember. Everything else is a blank." She looked up at him with her pretty green eyes. "Why can't I remember? I feel like I'm forgetting something important."

"Like someone shooting you point-blank in the chest?" T-Mac snorted. "That's something you might want to forget. Or maybe it's your mind's way of protecting you." He brought her hand up to his mouth and pressed a kiss to the back of her knuckles. "Don't let it worry you. When you're ready, you'll remember." He kissed her hand again before he even realized what he was doing.

Her gaze went from her hand to his face. "Why did you do that?"

Heat rose up his neck into his cheeks. "I don't know. I'm sorry. I shouldn't have." He laid her hand on the sheet. "Maybe I should go."

"No." She reached out and snagged his fingers with hers. "Please, don't go. Unless you have to." Her cheeks flushed. "I didn't say I didn't like it."

"Yeah, well, I shouldn't have done it anyway. I don't know why, but it just felt right." He held out his hand. "I'm sorry. It won't happen again."

An awkward silence ensued. One in which T-Mac couldn't look Kinsley in the eyes.

Finally, she squeezed his hand and let go. "I've kept you here long enough. I plan on sleeping until tomorrow and then initiating my escape plan."

T-Mac chuckled. "I'm sure Agar will be a big help in your endeavors." He stepped away from the bed and looked around. "If Agar is staying with you tonight, we need to see to his comfort as well as yours. I'll be right back."

He turned away, kicking himself for kissing the woman's hand. What if a nurse or doctor had walked in? He was taking advantage of the woman when she was at her most vulnerable. And worse, his actions could have been construed as fraternization, which could not only get him in trouble, but Kinsley as well.

T-Mac searched through the cabinet in the room. He found a bedpan and some kind of sterile bowl. He pulled the bowl off a shelf, filled it with water from the sink in the adjoining bathroom and set it on the floor.

Agar leaped down from the bed, trotted over to the bowl of water and licked it dry.

T-Mac chuckled. "Hey, boy, you must have been really thirsty."

"I swear that dog is part camel." Kinsley laughed. "I keep expecting him to grow a hump from all the water he consumes."

Squatting next to the dog, T-Mac rubbed the animal behind the ears. "You're lucky to have Agar."

"I know," Kinsley said, her voice low. "I'm sick that I almost lost him."

T-Mac glanced up to catch Kinsley staring at him. Not the dog. His pulse pushed blood through his veins at an alarming speed. He didn't know what was wrong with him, but if he didn't leave soon, he'd do more than just kiss the woman's hand. And he couldn't let that happen. "I'm sorry, but I have to go."

She nodded. "I know. You can't babysit the dog handler forever."

He turned to leave.

"T-Mac." Kinsley's voice stopped him from making good his escape.

He made the mistake of turning back.

Kinsley lay against the sheets looking small and vulnerable.

"Yes?" T-Mac kept his distance, while clenching his fists to keep from reaching out to take her into his arms.

"You're an amazing man. Thank you for rescuing me."

"Don't mention it," he said, and left the room.

Chapter Five

The nurses and the doctor who visited Kinsley throughout the rest of the day and into the night didn't seem at all put out by Agar's presence. Kinsley suspected T-Mac had something to do with their casual acceptance. And for that she was grateful.

Having Agar with her helped her make it through the nightmares that woke her several times in a single hour.

At one point, she woke up calling out T-Mac's name. When she realized what she'd done, she looked around quickly, hoping no one else had heard. Once she ascertained she was well and truly alone, she was able to relax. At the same time, she missed having the navy SEAL there in her room, holding her hand. And, if she were honest with herself, she wanted him to kiss her again. But not on her hand.

The sun and Agar's soft whining woke Kinsley the next morning. She rolled out of the narrow bed and landed on her bare feet. The cool tile flooring against her toes and the draft through the back of her gown made her shiver.

Agar danced beside her, ready to go outside for his morning run.

"Sorry, boy, we have to get permission from the doctor."

"Speak of the devil…" The doctor entered the room. "And here I am." He chuckled at his own joke and then got serious. "Headache?" The doctor pulled a penlight from his breast pocket.

"No, sir."

He shone the light into her eyes. "Dizziness?"

"No, sir."

"How are those ribs?" He patted his hand on the bed. "Hop up and let me look you over."

"The ribs are mildly sore, but livable." She scooted her bottom onto the edge of the bed and swung her legs up.

"Lie down on the bed," the doctor ordered.

After a nurse joined them in the room, the doc lifted her gown to inspect the bruising on her ribs, pushing here and there until he was satisfied nothing was broken.

Kinsley bit down hard on her tongue to keep from crying out a couple of times. It hurt, but she refused to be put on profile until the bruising went away. She wanted to get back out and make sure no one triggered an unexpected explosion and lost lives or limbs. She and Agar had a job to do, and by God, they were going to do it.

"As much as I'd like to keep you and have someone for my staff to work on, I can't find enough wrong with you."

Kinsley sat up, grinning. "Really?"

"The nurse will give you discharge instructions."

"So, I can return to duty?"

The doctor held up a single finger. "Light duty for a day, to make sure you don't have any residual effects of the explosion or gunshot."

"Thank you." Kinsley was so relieved she wanted to cry.

Agar's tail pounded the floor beside the bed.

"I'm really releasing you to get this hairy beast out of my facility." The doctor brushed a dog hair from his white coat. "Now, get out of here before I change my mind."

"I will." Kinsley hopped off the bed, grabbed Agar's lead and made for the door.

"Eh-hem." The doctor cleared his throat. "Aren't you forgetting something?"

The cool tile beneath her feet and the draft on her backside made a rush of heat climb up her cheeks. Her heart sank. "I don't suppose I can borrow some scrubs or something?"

"As a matter of fact, I have what you need." The nurse reentered the room carrying a stack of clothing. "A handsome navy SEAL delivered these this morning for you. He apologized about the size but said he didn't have access to your room to get your own things." She grinned.

Kinsley took the shorts, T-shirt and socks from the woman. "These will do."

"Let me know if you need any help," she offered.

"Thank you."

Once the doctor and nurse left the room, Kinsley stripped out of the gown and pulled the T-shirt over her head. The hem fell down around her knees. Undaunted, she slipped into the shorts and dragged them up over her hips. They were too big, but she was able to tighten the string at the waist to keep them from falling off.

The heels of the socks came halfway up her ankles, but they were fine to get her to her quarters. She found her boots in the corner and pulled them on. Feeling like an orphan in hand-me-downs, she grabbed Agar's leash and headed out of the medical facility and across the compound to the containerized living units.

Agar trotted alongside her, his steps light, tail wagging. Thankfully, he seemed to have no ill effects from his own brush with death.

As she walked past the motor pool, a man in an army uniform smiled and waved in her direction.

Kinsley nodded and waved back.

Another man stood on the front bumper of one of the big trucks, leaning over the open engine. He raised his head for moment but didn't acknowledge her. Instead, his gaze followed her.

Agar growled.

"I agree. He wasn't very friendly," Kinsley whispered, and walked faster until she moved out of sight of the motor pool.

As she passed by the command center, the navy commander who'd called for the mission that had almost gotten her killed stepped out of the building. "Ah, Specialist Anderson. I'm glad to see you up and about." His gaze swept over her outfit.

Kinsley lifted her chin. "I was just released from the medical facility. I'm on my way to my quarters to change into a uniform."

The commander's brow dipped. "Should you return to work so soon?"

"I'm on light duty for a day, then I'm back to regular duty." She motioned for Agar to sit. "I wanted to let you know I'm ready and able to perform my mission, should you need me."

"Good to know. I might have something coming up soon. I'll keep you in mind."

"Thank you, sir," she said.

"Can I interest you in some fabulous food from our neighborhood chow hall?" He waved his hand toward the dining facility. "I'm headed there now."

"No, thank you, sir," Kinsley said. "I need to change and exercise Agar."

"Don't overdo it," the commander said.

"Yes, sir." Kinsley hurried along, determined to reach her quarters before she encountered anyone else. She didn't like being out of uniform in the oversize shirt and shorts, looking goofy in a pair of combat boots. She'd seen worse while she'd been there, but she held herself to a higher standard. And she was grateful for the clothing to get across the compound. She couldn't imagine traipsing across Camp Lemonnier in nothing but boots and a hospital gown.

Thankfully, she didn't encounter anyone else on her way to her quarters. Her skin crawled with a strange feeling someone was watching her. She flung open the door.

Agar stepped inside.

Then Kinsley slipped into the shipping container, closed the door behind her and stood for a moment, listening for footsteps outside.

The crunch of gravel sent a shiver along her spine.

Agar pressed his nose to the door crack and sniffed. Then he sniffed again, his hackles rising.

Kinsley knew she should look outside and see who was there, but she couldn't bring herself to do it.

Then, as quickly as Agar's hackles rose, they fell back in place and he trotted over to her bed and lay down.

"What was all that about?" Kinsley asked.

When the dog looked up at her from his lounging position on the floor, he cocked his head to one side.

"You're hopeless." Kinsley yanked off the T-shirt that smelled amazingly like T-Mac. She pressed it to her nose, inhaled his scent and tossed the shirt on the bed.

The shorts were next.

Wanting to prove she was up to working again, Kinsley changed into a clean uniform, brushed her hair and pulled it back into a tight bun at the nape of her neck. Sore around the stitches on her leg and achy around the ribs, she didn't slow down, but called for Agar. She snatched up his lead, his KONG and the training aid she used with the trace scent of explosives inside.

Agar leaped to his feet as soon as he saw the dog toy. He loved chewing on the KONG and would do almost anything she asked just to get to play with it for a few seconds.

Feeling a little more like normal, if somewhat beaten up, Kinsley left her quarters and walked out to the camp trash containers. With the sun rising high in the sky, barely a breeze to stir the air and the sun's heating the earth and the trash, the smell was barely tolerable and perfect to help disguise the training aid.

Kinsley tied Agar to a post and then ducked between trash bins to hide the toy.

When she returned, Agar's ears perked. She gave him the signal to find the explosives and let him out to the end of his lead.

Within minutes, he found the aid. Kinsley's heart swelled and she praised the dog for his find. She rewarded him by throwing his KONG and letting him run to fetch it. Repeating the exercise several more times, she was satisfied Agar hadn't lost his touch. She took him for a long walk around the perimeter of the camp, hoping to stretch the kinks out of her body and work thoughts of a certain navy SEAL out of her mind.

She'd have to return his clothes soon, and the thought warmed her all the way to her core. Which scared the crap out of her. She did *not* need to get involved with a navy guy. Nothing could come of it. They were both committed to their military careers.

Besides, nothing could happen while they were deployed together. And when they returned stateside, he'd end up in some navy base on the East or West Coast and she'd be at an army post, probably in the middle of the country, like Texas or Oklahoma. They might as well be on different continents.

The sooner she got the man out of her head, the better. But the more she walked, the more she thought about Petty Officer Trace McGuire. The man with the strong hands and big heart, who'd rescued her when she'd been knocked down and stayed by her side in recovery.

AFTER A TERRIBLE sleepless night, T-Mac left his bed early and went for a run around Camp Lemonnier. Then he hit the weight room for forty brutal minutes pumping iron. And he still couldn't get Kinsley out of his head.

He'd purposely resisted going straight to the medical facility and checking on her. But the longer he stayed away, the more he wanted to go. He showered, put on a fresh uniform and stepped out of his quarters. Despite his effort to stay away, his feet carried him to the medical facility. The closer he got, the faster he walked until he burst through the door.

He didn't stop to say anything to the guy at the desk, but kept walking straight to Specialist Anderson's room. About to barge in, he stopped himself short and forced calm into his fist as he knocked.

When no one answered, he knocked again. Was she asleep?

When no one answered the second time, he pushed open the door and marched in.

The bed was freshly made and completely empty.

Damn! Where had she gone?

"Specialist Anderson was discharged first thing this morning," a voice said behind him.

He turned to face the nurse who'd checked on Kinsley the day before.

"Is she well enough?"

The woman smiled. "She was. The doctor signed her release papers. She practically ran out the door with her dog. Oh, by the way, thank you for bringing the clothes. I think she would have walked out of here in her boots and the hospital gown if she hadn't had them to change into."

A smile tugged at the corners of T-Mac's mouth. "I'm sure she was happy to be free."

The nurse's lips twisted. "It's not like we're a prison in here."

He chuckled. "No. And thank you for taking such good care of us."

She nodded. "Not many guys have the patience or desire to sit in a hospital room for hours on end. She's lucky to have you."

T-Mac didn't try to correct the woman. Kinsley didn't have him. He'd just done the right thing to take care of a fallen comrade. Nothing more.

"Thanks again," he said, and turned to leave.

"Do you want us to check your stitches?" the nurse asked. "We don't often get shrapnel wounds here. Most people come in with colds, allergies or the occasional broken bone from playing volleyball or football."

"No, thank you. You all did a good job. It's healing nicely," he said as he turned to leave. He didn't want to stand around and chitchat. He wanted to find Kinsley and see for himself that she was well enough to be back on her feet.

His first stop was her quarters. Once again, he knocked. No one answered.

When he raised his hand to knock again, someone spoke behind him.

"T-Mac, there you are. I've been looking all over for you."

T-Mac turned to find Harm standing behind him. The SEAL wore his desert-camouflage uniform and a floppy boonie hat instead of his Kevlar helmet.

"What's up?" T-Mac asked.

"The CO wants us in the command center for a briefing in fifteen minutes. I'm headed there now."

His fists tightening, T-Mac sighed. So much for finding Kinsley. He'd have to wait until after the briefing.

T-Mac fell in step beside Harm.

"How's your dog handler this morning?" Harm kicked a pebble in front of them.

"The doc released her." He didn't tell him that he wanted to see her and had yet to find her. Harm didn't need to know how the dog handler had him tied in knots. He'd get a big kick out of it and razz him even more than he already did.

"Glad to hear it," Harm said. "When will she be able to return to duty?"

"Tomorrow." Too soon, by T-Mac's standards.

"What about the dog?"

"Agar spent the night with her at the medical facility. He seemed to be no worse for the wear."

"Good to hear. We might need them on the next mission."

"We've done just fine on most missions without a bomb-sniffing dog."

"What? You don't want Anderson and Agar in the heat of things with us?"

"Not really."

Harm grinned. "You really like her, don't you?"

"I didn't say that," he grumbled. "I just think she's a distraction we can ill afford."

"There's probably a little truth in that statement." Harm glanced toward the command center. "You were quick to load her up and get her out of there without looking back."

"My point exactly." T-Mac stopped in front of the building. "Don't you dare tell her I said that. She'd skin me alive if she knew I didn't want her on a mission."

"Too late," a female voice said behind him. "So, you don't want me on a mission?"

T-Mac balled his fists, dragged in a deep breath and turned to do damage control with Kinsley.

"Look, Kin—Specialist Anderson, I didn't say you weren't good at your job. I'm just saying that we're used to working as a combat team. The night before last was the first time we've integrated a dog team in a mission. And, well, you know what happened. It wasn't a raging success."

"And that was my fault?" she asked.

"If you hadn't been there…" T-Mac started.

Harm cleared his throat. "You might reconsider going there, buddy."

Kinsley held up a hand. "No, let him go. I want to know how deep he'll dig his own grave."

Anger rose up inside T-Mac, and he plowed right into waters he knew would be over his head in the next few words out of his mouth. "If you hadn't been there, one of us would have breached that building in a way we've been taught that doesn't involve walking through the door as if we expect a big hug and a hallelujah."

Her eyes narrowed. "And you think that's what I was doing?"

Harm crossed his arms over his chest and shook his head. "Told you to think before you opened your mouth." He held up his hands. "Now you're on your own. I'll see you two inside." Harm bailed on T-Mac and entered the command center.

"So, you think I don't know what I'm doing?" Kinsley asked.

"I think you're more concerned about your dog than your own life."

"Maybe you're right. I care about Agar." Her chin lifted even higher. "At least I care about someone."

"I'm sure you and Agar are good at sniffing out IEDs and land mines, but clearing buildings might not be the right fit for you."

Kinsley's face grew redder and redder. "It's a good thing you're not my boss, or anywhere in my chain of command. Now, if you'll excuse me, I've been summoned for a job. A job you don't think I can do." She spun on her heel and marched into the command center without looking back.

Once again, T-Mac could kick himself for opening his big mouth. The woman had a right to be spitting mad at him. He just couldn't see going through what he'd been through two nights ago again.

When Kinsley had been blown out of that hut and lay on the ground like she had, T-Mac's heart had stopped and then turned flips trying to restart and propel him forward to pick up the pieces. What had him all wound up was the possibility that next time, Kinsley might not be as lucky. She might actually be in pieces. And he didn't want to be the one to pick them up.

Chapter Six

Kinsley stood in the command-center war room, too mad to sit. How dare T-Mac tell his teammate he didn't want her on another mission?

Hadn't she and Agar gotten them through a minefield upon entering the abandoned village?

The CO paced at the front of the room, waiting for everyone to enter and take a seat. He raised his brow at Kinsley, who still stood. "Please, take a seat."

"Sir, if you don't mind, I'd prefer to stand," Kinsley said. The only empty seat happened to be beside T-Mac. And she sure as hell wasn't going to sit next to him. Not when he'd impugned her honor and spread doubt about her abilities as a dog handler and soldier.

"Suit yourself," the commander said. He addressed Kinsley and the room full of SEALs. "The mission two nights ago didn't go the way we expected."

Several snorts were emitted by various members of the SEAL team.

Kinsley held her tongue.

"We were lucky to come out with as few casualties as we did," the commander continued. "As it is, having Specialist Anderson join the effort was a welcome addition to the team. Without her, our SEALs might have stepped on and triggered half a dozen or more mines on their way into the village where the arms trading was to take place." He held up a hand. "I know I'm repeating old news, but I want to be clear… We cannot have a repeat of what happened that night."

"Sir, does that mean we're going out again?" Big Jake asked.

"I'm not sure you are," the CO said. "But the rest of the team is going."

Big Jake placed both hands flat on the table. "Sir, I might have taken a hit in the rear, but the rest of me works just fine. I won't be sitting on a mission. And where my guys go, I go."

The CO stared hard at Big Jake. "If you think you're up to it."

"I am, sir," Big Jake said without hesitation.

"Good." He stared around the room again. "What happened two nights ago was an ambush. They knew you were coming and they were waiting for you to enter the village before they attacked."

Kinsley gasped. Having been in the hospital since the incident, and being the only army personnel in a sea of navy SEALs, she hadn't been included in the scuttlebutt. "You think we were set up?"

The commander nodded. "Someone leaked information about the mission. We still don't know who did it, but we suspect it's someone here on Camp Lemonnier."

Kinsley glanced around the table of men, all loyal, career military men who'd risked their lives on many occasions for their country. "You don't think it was anyone in this room, do you?"

"No, not anyone in this room," the commander said.

"I should think not," Kinsley said.

T-Mac's lips twitched, as did others in the room.

"We have a traitor amongst us on Camp Lemonnier. And that traitor is quite possibly connected to the illegal arms trading going on."

"What's being done about it?" Harm asked.

"We've interviewed everyone involved with the helicopters. We don't know for certain, but we don't believe any of them were the culprit." The commander sighed. "And if one of them is, we haven't found the connection yet."

He paused for a moment before continuing.

"But we can't sit back and wait until we find him. We have new intel, and we need to move on it before it becomes useless."

The SEALs all leaned forward in their chairs.

"We have infrared satellite images from two nights ago. When our guys bugged out of that village that night, two trucks left in the opposite direction." The CO stared around the room. "Bottom line is, we know where they went."

"Where?" Kinsley asked.

The commander shook his head. "I can't say. Until we launch a mission, I'm not revealing any specifics about any part of that mission until the choppers are off the ground."

"Radio signals can be intercepted," T-Mac said.

"I didn't say I was going to use radio signals."

Pitbull frowned. "Then how will we know where we're going?"

The commander stared around the room. "I'm going with you. I will have the mission-specific information necessary to carry out the assignment."

"Sir, you haven't trained with the team," Buck pointed out.

"Won't that make the mission higher profile?" Big Jake asked. "If someone is leaking information and learns you're going along for the ride, won't that make the rest of us collateral damage when they're targeting you?"

"First of all," the commander said, "this information is not to go outside this room. No one other than the people here are to know we have intel on a potential location of the attackers from the village the other night. No one outside this room should know what we know. Not the helicopter pilots, the mechanics, anyone in the mess hall or anywhere else."

The commander continued. "Every one of you should be ready to go at a moment's notice. When we take off, you will have only a few minutes to prepare. Can you be ready?"

"Sir, yes, sir!" Kinsley shouted along with the SEAL team.

"Then for now, not a word to anyone." The commander's eyes narrowed. "Not even to each other. We can't risk being overheard. Understood?"

Kinsley stood at attention and shouted, "Sir, yes, sir!" along with the others in the room.

The commander nodded, apparently satisfied. "Then you're all dismissed until further notice."

One by one, the SEALs filed out of the room but without the usual banter.

Kinsley stood in the corner, waiting until the others were gone. Then she and Agar approached the commander. "Sir, do you still plan on using me and Agar in the next mission?"

"Specialist Anderson, I would not have allowed you in the room with the others if I didn't plan on taking you along." He stared hard into her eyes. "Are you up to another mission so soon?"

She nodded. "Yes, sir."

"That's all I need to know. You proved invaluable on the last one. I see no reason to leave you out of the next one."

"Thank you, sir."

"You realize that some of the men might consider you a distraction to the mission."

Her blood pressure rocketed and her jaw tightened. "Did T-Mac say that?"

"Not actually." The commander smiled. "His report to me was that you were fearless." His smile turned into a frown. "Why? Are you and T-Mac at odds? Do you want me to assign a different SEAL to look out for you?"

Fearless? He thought she was fearless? And yet, he didn't want her on a mission.

"I could get Harm or Buck to look out for you," the commander offered.

"No," Kinsley said, her pulse racing. "T-Mac was there for me. I trust him." And she did. She'd bet her life on him. But was she betting his life on her being a part of the mission? Was it right for her to want to go even though she was a distraction to them?

She stiffened her spine and pulled back her shoulders. Based on what had happened on the last mission, and finding all those land mines buried along the path the SEALs were destined to follow, she had to go. Whoever would set those up the way they had could do it again.

Not only did she want to go, she *had* to go. Otherwise, she would be sitting back at Camp Lemonnier, safe and sound, while the SEAL team could be walking into a minefield. They needed her and Agar. She had to be with them. If something happened to them that she and Agar could have helped them avoid, she could never live with herself.

She looked the commander square in the eye. "Sir, I'm ready whenever you are. Just say the word."

He nodded. "That's what I wanted to hear."

"WALK WITH ME," Harm said as they left the command center.

T-Mac would rather have waited for Kinsley, but he didn't want to admit it, so he fell in step beside Harm.

Instead of turning toward their quarters, he headed toward the flight line where the helicopters were parked.

"You know you can't always protect her, don't you?" Harm said.

T-Mac knew it would serve no purpose to pretend he didn't know who Harm was talking about. "Who said I always want to protect her?"

Harm stopped short of the helicopters and stood staring at them. "She's special. I didn't expect her to be so brave about sniffing out land mines."

His lips twitching, T-Mac rolled his eyes. "She doesn't sniff out the mines. Agar does."

"You know what I mean."

"Yeah, I do. You should have seen her go after Agar when he ran into that hut." The image was etched indelibly into T-Mac's mind. "And then watch as she was blown back out by the force of the bullet that hit her vest."

Harm laid a hand on T-Mac's shoulder. "That shook you, didn't it?"

"I've never been more shaken," T-Mac admitted.

"I know what you mean. We anticipate our own deaths and meet that possibility head-on. But when it comes to someone else, we have a more difficult time accepting or even processing it."

T-Mac nodded. "You hit the nail on the head. All I could think about was how to get her out of that place as quickly as possible. I would have felt the same had it been one of my teammates."

Harm snorted. "I know you would rush in to help if one of us was hit, but I think it was more than that with the dog handler."

A frown pulled T-Mac's brow downward. "Don't read more into my actions than what's there."

Harm held up his hands. "Just saying. You don't have to bite my head off."

"You and the others think that just because you have women, I need one, too. I don't need a woman in my life. And Specialist Anderson isn't that woman anyway."

"You don't think so?"

"I wouldn't know," T-Mac said. "We haven't known each other for very long."

"Speaking from my experience," Harm said, "it doesn't take long to fall in love. Sometimes you just know she's the one."

"Like you and Talia?" T-Mac asked.

"Yeah. Like me and Talia." Harm smiled as he stared at the helicopter. He was probably seeing Talia, the petite beauty with the black hair and blue eyes, not the smooth gray hulks of Black Hawk helicopters.

T-Mac shook his head. "How do you know?"

"At first, I didn't recognize it, but the more I was

around her, the more I wanted to be around her. And then when we were apart, all I could do was think about her."

That's not me. T-Mac refused to believe that was what he was feeling about Kinsley. Yeah, he'd seen her around camp. And he'd fantasized about getting to know her better, even how it would be to kiss her. But love?

Oh, hell no.

But, like Harm, he couldn't stop thinking about her and counted the minutes until he could see her again.

What was wrong with him? He did not need a woman in his life, despite what his buddies thought.

He turned away from the choppers. "We should go prepare."

Harm touched T-Mac's arm. "Falling for a woman is not a bad thing."

"I wouldn't know," T-Mac insisted.

"It doesn't make you weaker," Harm continued. "In fact, it makes me stronger, more determined to do the right thing and be a better person. The kind of person Talia would want to be with."

"Well, that certainly isn't me. Not with Kinsley. I told her I didn't want her to be on the next mission."

Harm's eyebrows shot up. "Kinsley?"

"Specialist Anderson," T-Mac corrected.

"That's why she looked mad enough to spit nails." Harm chuckled.

"Yeah." T-Mac started walking again. "She sure as hell doesn't want to be with me now."

"An apology goes a long way to smoothing a woman's feathers," Harm advised.

T-Mac shot a horrified glance his buddy's way. "Apologize? I'm not sorry I told her that. She's one hundred percent a distraction on a mission."

"Maybe for you, since you're into her."

"I'm not into her." He couldn't be. It made no sense.

"No? Then why did you spend the night at her bedside, holding her hand?" Harm raised an eyebrow. "And don't say you'd have done the same for one of us."

T-Mac opened his mouth to tell Harm that holding Kinsley's hand didn't mean anything, but he knew it would be a big fat lie. So he closed his mouth, sealed his lips in a thin, tight line and stepped out smartly for his quarters.

Harm jogged to catch up. "You can run, buddy, but you can't hide from the truth."

T-Mac came to an abrupt halt.

Harm ran into him.

"Let's get this straight." T-Mac turned and poked a finger into Harm's chest. "I'm not into Kinsley. We're not together. She's just an army puke with a dog. Nothing more. Period. The end."

Harm stared into T-Mac's eyes and then burst into laughter. "Damn, dude, you've got it really bad for the woman."

T-Mac balled his fists and cocked his arms.

The smile left Harm's face and he held up his hands. "Hey, remember me? I'm on *your* side."

Still ready to hit someone, T-Mac kept his fists up.

"All right. I'll stop razzing you." Harm dropped his hands and tipped his head toward the living quarters. "We'd better get ready. Who knows when we'll get the call?" He stepped out.

For a long moment, T-Mac stood with his hands up, jaw clenched and anger simmering. Finally, he let go of the breath he'd been holding and turned to follow his friend.

They were almost to the living units when T-Mac spoke again, as if they hadn't ended the conversation. "It doesn't matter anyway."

"What?" Harm asked.

"Nothing could ever come of something between us."

"Between who?" Harm grinned and jerked his thumb between T-Mac and himself. "You and me? You're right. I'm taken."

"Shut up. You know who I'm talking about."

Harm nodded. "Yeah, but I also know things have a way of working out."

"Like Talia's resort burning down so she's forced to move back to the States to be with you? Or Marly's airplane blowing up so she can move back to the States and be with Pitbull?"

With a frown, Harm kicked at a rock. "When

you put it like that, it sounds bad. But maybe there's something to fate."

"I don't wish anything ill on Kinsley or Agar. They've worked hard for what they do. If I was interested in Kinsley—which I'm not—I couldn't ask her to give up her career to follow me around. Nor would I want to give up my career to follow her. So it doesn't matter. Nothing could ever come of a relationship between me and Kinsley."

With a shrug, Harm opened the door to the quarters they shared and held it for T-Mac to enter. "All I know is, you never know."

T-Mac snorted. "Sounds like double-talk to me."

"Maybe. Maybe not. Just wait and see. If she's worth it, you'll find a way."

T-Mac went to work preparing for the next mission, not knowing what it would be, where they would go or how he'd make it through the tough times and keep Kinsley out of the line of fire. One thing he did know, but wouldn't admit to Harm or anyone else, was that Kinsley was definitely worth the trouble. She was brave, loyal and beautiful.

He cleaned his M4A1 rifle and his nine-millimeter handgun. Then he spent time sharpening his Ka-Bar knife and checking his communications equipment. When he was finished, he stood, stretched and asked, "Ready to hit the chow hall?"

Harm nodded. "Give me a minute to lay out my gear."

While Harm set out his body armor, helmet and night-vision goggles, T-Mac did the same.

By the time they finished, T-Mac's belly rumbled.

They left their quarters and walked toward the dining facility.

As T-Mac passed Kinsley's unit, he noticed a package sitting on the ground directly in front of her door. Wrapped in brown paper, it looked like something the postmaster might have delivered. Except the camp postmaster didn't make deliveries.

At that moment, Kinsley opened the door.

Agar started to step out on the ground and stopped. He sniffed the package once and lay down, blocking Kinsley's exit, his tongue hanging out, his gaze seeking her.

Kinsley nearly tripped over the dog, expecting him to exit. When he didn't, she looked past him to the package, her brow furrowing. She hesitated and stepped back into the unit. "Good boy, Agar. Good boy."

T-Mac stared from the dog to the package and back again. "Did you place that package there?" he asked.

Kinsley's gaze locked with T-Mac's, her eyes going wide. "I was going to ask you the same question."

"Don't bother." T-Mac turned to his friend. "Harm, get back to the command center and report a potential bomb located inside the perimeter."

Harm nodded. "On it." He turned and ran back in the direction from which they'd come.

"Is Agar ever wrong?" T-Mac asked.

Kinsley shook her head. "He tests out at one hundred percent, even with trace amounts of explosives in the decoy."

"Can you step around it?" T-Mac asked.

"Probably?"

T-Mac moved closer to the package and held out his arms. "You can lean on my shoulders and I can help you out."

"No," she said.

With a frown, T-Mac dropped his arms. "No, you can't? Or no, you won't?"

"No, I won't leave Agar." Her lips pressed into a straight line.

"Step back—I'm coming to you."

Her eyes widened. "No! You can't. What if it explodes?"

"Then we'll go together." He winked. "Won't that be romantic or something?"

"Are you insane?" She held up her hands. "I'm going inside the unit and closing the door. Let me know when the unexploded-ordnance guys are done." She backed up a step, held the door wide and called to Agar to follow.

Agar rose and entered the unit, trotting past Kinsley.

When Kinsley stepped back and started to close the door, T-Mac made his move. He took a giant step over the package and fell through the door frame.

"What the—" Kinsley said as he caught her around the waist and took her to the ground with him.

With his foot, T-Mac kicked the door shut behind him and covered Kinsley's body with his own.

He waited for several long minutes, trying to shield Kinsley from the shrapnel sure to pepper their bodies should the package explode.

After three minutes passed, Kinsley stirred beneath him. "T-Mac," she said, her voice barely a whisper.

"Yes?"

"What are you doing?" Kinsley breathed.

"Saving your life."

"Is that what this is?" Her breathing came in short, shallow gasps.

"Of course."

"Sweetheart, you're killing me," she wheezed.

Sweetheart? Had she really called him *sweetheart?* His chest swelled and warmth spread throughout his body from every point of contact with hers. Which was practically everywhere. All that warmth pooled low in his groin. And his body reacted to the heat and he grew hard.

"T-Mac?" Kinsley said.

"Mmm," he murmured.

"I can't breathe," she whispered.

Immediately, he rose up on his elbows, giving her chest the space she needed to take a deep breath and fill her lungs. "Sorry."

"It's okay. I didn't die." She chuckled. "And the package didn't explode."

"No. But we don't know if it will. What if whoever put it there can trigger it to explode at any time?"

"I would think he would have triggered it when I opened the door."

"Maybe, or maybe he's waiting for a bigger crowd. In which case you won't be safe until the ordnance-disposal guys arrive."

"We can't lie here for that long," she said, her voice all practical but still a little breathless.

T-Mac refused to move. He couldn't risk leaving her exposed. "What does it hurt to stay put for a little longer?"

"I don't want you to shield my body with yours. The navy put a lot of training into you."

"And the army put a lot of training into you and Agar. Speaking of which…can you get him to lie down in case the explosives go off? I'd hate for either one of you to be injured."

"Agar, lie down," she commanded.

The dog dropped to his belly beside Kinsley.

She stared up into T-Mac's eyes. "So, does this mean you care?"

T-Mac frowned. "Only because my commander put me in charge of making sure you're okay."

"Really?" She tilted her head. "That's the only reason?"

"Of course."

Her pretty, peach-pink lips twisted. "Your commander tasked you with that responsibility during our last mission," Kinsley pointed out. "We're not on that mission now."

"I take my responsibilities seriously," T-Mac argued, refusing to admit that he probably would have protected her even if his commander hadn't tasked him with the job. Something about Kinsley drew him, and like a moth to the flame, he couldn't resist. And like that moth, he figured he'd eventually be burned in some way or another. Navy SEALs, by the nature of their work, were doomed in the relationship department.

But at that moment, when they faced the possibility of being blown to bits, he stared down into her face, his gaze zeroing in on her pouty lips.

And he couldn't resist.

He leaned down, his mouth hovering over hers. "I take my responsibilities very seriously," he repeated.

"T-Mac?" Kinsley's breath warmed his mouth. "Are you going to kiss me?"

He nodded. "Yup. Do you have a problem with that?"

"Yes," she said, her voice a hot puff of air against his lips. "You're taking too long."

He claimed her mouth in a long, hard kiss that shook him to his very core. She wrapped her arms around his neck, her fingers threading into the hair at the back of his neck and pulling him closer.

When he ran his tongue across the seam of her lips, she opened to him.

He dove in, deepening the kiss, sliding his tongue along hers in a warm, wet caress, one he never wanted to end.

Kinsley wrapped her calf around his and pushed her hips up, making him even harder.

By the time he raised his head, his body was on fire and he couldn't get enough of her.

He rested his forehead against hers and dragged in air. "What the hell just happened?"

Kinsley chuckled and her breath hitched. "You tell me."

T-Mac brushed his lips across hers in a feather-light kiss. He couldn't get over how soft they were, or that she tasted of mint.

Agar crawled forward and laid his head on Kinsley's shoulder.

Laughter bubbled up in T-Mac's chest. Despite the fact there was a bomb outside the container unit, he'd never felt so light. All because he'd kissed Kinsley.

"T-Mac?" Harm's voice called to him from outside the container. "Are you two in there?"

"If we're really quiet, do you think they'll go away?" Kinsley asked.

T-Mac liked that she could joke when the circumstances could go south quickly. "I doubt it."

"Well, damn." She cupped his cheeks between her palms, leaned her head up and pressed a hard kiss to his mouth. "Then you'd better answer."

He drew in a deep breath, every movement reminding him he was lying on top of a female with curves in all the right places. "We're in here," T-Mac called out.

"Hang tight," Harm said. "The EOD guys are going to remove the package. Stay down."

"Will do," T-Mac said, his gaze never moving from Kinsley's.

"I don't like that you're not wearing body armor," she said.

"I'm liking that I'm not. A little too much." His shaft pressed into her pelvis. He shifted his body to ease the pressure.

Kinsley's eyes flared and her hips rose as if seeking to reestablish the connection. Then she dropped her bottom back to the floor. "You should probably move." Her voice sounded as if she'd been running, her chest rising and falling in shallow breaths.

"Sorry, sweetheart," T-Mac said. "I'm not moving until the danger's over."

"I'm not sure where it's most dangerous…outside my door, or in here." She held his gaze.

"Specialist Anderson, are you afraid of me?" he asked, his tone deep, his body humming with a rush of heat.

"No, Petty Officer McGuire." Her gaze shifted from his eyes to his lips. "I'm afraid of me."

Chapter Seven

Lying sandwiched between the hard metal floor of the container unit and the muscular planes of T-Mac's chest, torso, hips and thighs, Kinsley could barely breathe. And it had nothing to do with T-Mac crushing her chest. He'd removed his weight, balancing over her on his arms.

The man stole her breath away by his sheer alpha maleness.

He could have run away from the package of explosives on her doorstep and left her and Agar to whatever happened.

But he hadn't. He'd sacrificed his own safety to protect her.

Kinsley's estimation of the man increased tenfold. Hell, he'd already proven he could rescue her from tight situations.

But when he'd kissed her…

Sweet, sweet heaven. He'd changed everything in just that one meeting of their lips.

Now she couldn't stop thinking about him and really wished he'd kiss her again.

He lowered his head, his gaze shifting from her eyes to her lips. "This could get us in trouble."

"Big trouble," she whispered, her lips tingling in anticipation of his.

"Hang in there, T-Mac. They're moving the package now." Harm's muffled shout reached her through the walls of her quarters.

They had only seconds to live if the explosives detonated. Or seconds to kiss if they didn't.

Kinsley didn't want to die without just one more...

She reached up, her hand circling the back of T-Mac's head, and pulled him down to her mouth.

She'd never felt so empowered and yet vulnerable as she did in that one desperate kiss.

"They're gone!" Harm shouted.

The rattle of the doorknob alerted Kinsley to impending danger. She planted her hands on T-Mac's chest and shoved him over.

He went willingly, springing to his feet just as the door swung open.

"EOD saved the day," Harm said.

T-Mac reached out a hand. Kinsley placed hers in his and let him bring her to her feet to face T-Mac's friend.

"Are you all right?" Harm asked, his gaze slipping over her face and narrowing in on her lips.

She nodded, her cheeks heating. Could he tell she'd just been kissed? Kinsley fought the urge to press her palms to her cheeks and further incriminate herself. No one had seen what had happened between her and T-Mac. No one had to know. She didn't need an Article 15 on her record. She could lose her position as a dog handler.

Command Order number one when deployed was No Fraternization.

And she'd just fraternized.

She shot a glace toward T-Mac. His gaze was on her, making her entire body burn with desire. What was it about this man that made her feel completely out of control?

"What was in the package?" T-Mac asked.

"We won't know until the EOD guys can either dismantle it or blow it up. I suspect they'll blow it up. Either way, they'll let us know."

T-Mac's lips pressed into a thin line and his jaw firmed. "What the hell? We're inside the wire here in Djibouti."

Harm nodded. "Which means we have a traitor among us."

"Someone who doesn't like me," Kinsley added.

"Why?" Harm asked.

"My guess is whoever left the package could be the one who shot Kinsley point-blank." T-Mac's chest tightened. "He's afraid she'll recognize him and blow his cover."

"But I can't remember anything about that incident," Kinsley said.

"He probably knows that," Harm said. "Word gets around camp quickly."

"He probably also knows that your memory could return at any time. He just wants to make sure it doesn't happen before he can get rid of you." T-Mac faced Kinsley. "Until we determine who it is, you're not safe here."

A shiver rippled from the base of Kinsley's neck down her spine. "In that case, we might as well go on another mission. Agar and I will be as safe, if not safer, with your SEAL team."

"True," Harm said.

T-Mac's jaw tightened.

Kinsley almost laughed. The man was torn. He didn't want her on any mission with them, but she could tell he didn't like the idea of her staying behind and being the target of a traitor.

Finally, he sighed. "You're right. In the meantime, I'm hanging out with Specialist Anderson until further notice."

"You know you can't stay in her quarters," Harm reminded him.

"I know, but I sure as hell can camp out on her doorstep."

"I don't need a babysitter," Kinsley insisted.

"No, but you need a bodyguard." T-Mac held up a hand to keep her from saying more. "Just go with this. If this were happening to one of us, we'd do the same."

Harm nodded. "That's true. You always need someone watching your back."

T-Mac winked. "I've got your six. Think about it. If Agar hadn't warned you, what would have happened?"

A chill swept across her skin. She could have been blown to bits.

"Come on." Harm jerked his head toward the command center. "We need to report to the CO. He has to know what just happened."

Agar nudged her hand.

Kinsley rubbed her fingers over the top of his head. "It's okay, boy." Then she snapped on his lead. He couldn't know all of what was happening, but he was unsettled by the number of people in her quarters and Kinsley's physical distress, no matter how she tried to hide it.

T-Mac and Harm marched her to the command center. The other four members of T-Mac's immediate team joined them, asking questions and expressing concern.

Once they reported what had happened to the commander, his face appeared as if set in stone. "We knew we had a possible leak among us, but this takes it to a different level." He nodded toward T-Mac. "You know what you have to do?"

T-Mac nodded. "I'll cover for Specialist Anderson."

"We'll all look out for her and Agar," Harm promised.

"Good." The commander glanced around at the

rest of the team. "We all need to be ready and keep our eyes peeled for anything that might lead us to our traitor."

All six SEALs and Kinsley snapped to attention. "Yes, sir!"

The commander touched Kinsley's arm. "Are you good with all this? If not, we can ship you out on the next transport."

"No way," she said, and added, "Sir. I'm in this for the long haul. Whoever is betraying us and our country needs to be brought down. I want to be a part of the takedown. That bastard needs to pay."

The commander grinned. "That's what I like to hear." He clapped his hands together. "Be alert. Be ready."

As they left the command center, Harm asked, "Anyone up for chow?"

"I'm not particularly hungry," Kinsley said.

"Yeah, but you need to fuel up," T-Mac said. "We never know when we'll be called up."

She nodded, knowing he was right. Her stomach was still knotted from the scare of the explosives package and the kiss from the man at her side. She wasn't sure any food would help her stomach relax, but she had to maintain her strength in order to keep up with the SEAL team. Kinsley refused to slow them down in any way.

In the dining facility, she choked down half a sandwich and a few chips and waited while the others finished their meals. By the time they were done, day was turning into evening.

They exited the dining facility and headed toward the living quarters.

Harm, Buck, Diesel, Big Jake and Pitbull peeled off at their quarters, but T-Mac continued beside Kinsley.

"Agar and I are going for a run. You don't have to go with us. We'll be out in the open and safe."

"I need to go for a run, too." He patted his flat abs. "Can't keep up my girlish figure by eating bonbons and sitting around."

"Seriously, I don't want to monopolize your time. Surely whoever left the package won't try anything out in broad—" she caught herself and continued "—out in the open."

"We don't know what he'll try. And if it's all right by you, I'm not taking any chances."

Kinsley sighed. "I don't like taking up all of your time."

"What else do we have to do?" He waved his hand at their surroundings. "It's the typical military deal— hurry up and wait."

"In that case, meet me outside in five minutes."

He planted his feet in the dirt and crossed his arms over his chest. "I'll wait here."

"No, really." Kinsley touched his arm and immediately retracted her hand when sparks seemed to fly off her fingers and up into her chest. "What could happen in five minutes?"

"A lot."

"You can't go with me everywhere, and I can't go with you. Five minutes will be fine." She pointed toward his unit. "Go change into your PT uniform."

"I'm wearing it," he insisted, though he was in his full uniform, boots and all.

Kinsley planted her fists on her hips. "I'm not going anywhere until you change into your shorts. And I'd have to wait for you outside your unit if I followed you. Just do it, and get back. I promise not to get blown up in the meantime."

He stood for a moment longer, staring into her eyes, and then sighed. "Okay, but I want to check your room before you go in."

Kinsley glanced down at her dog. "Agar does a pretty good job of it for me," she reminded him.

"Humor me, will ya?"

She raised her hands. "Okay." Unlocking the door, she pushed it open and released Agar's lead. "But let Agar go first."

T-Mac's lips twisted. "Deal."

She gave Agar the command to search, pointing into the building.

Agar entered, nose to the ground. As small as the unit was, it took only seconds for him to trot back to her side. He displayed no behavioral signs that anything might contain explosives.

She nodded toward T-Mac. "Your turn."

The navy SEAL entered the small box of a room

and searched high and low. What he was looking for, Kinsley had no clue.

When he returned to the door, she raised an eyebrow. "Find anything?" she asked, knowing the answer.

His eyes narrowed. "Don't get smart with me, Specialist."

Her eyes widened as she feigned innocence. "Me? Never."

T-Mac's lips curled on the corners and he lowered his voice until only she could hear him. "Don't tempt me to kiss you again."

Her heart fluttered. "Never," she whispered. Although, at that moment, she'd give anything to feel his lips on hers again. But they weren't locked behind a door, away from prying eyes, with the chance of a deadly explosion threatening to take their lives.

"Five minutes," she whispered.

"Close the door behind me," he said, and stepped out of the doorway.

Kinsley entered and closed the door behind her. Then she leaned against it and dragged in a deep breath. The man made her forget to breathe.

Agar nudged her hand, bringing her back to reality and the need to change quickly.

She rushed around the small space, tossing off her jacket and desert-tan T-shirt. She pulled on her army PT shirt, untied her boots and kicked them off. In short order, she switched her uniform trousers for shorts and her boots for running shoes.

A knock sounded as she pulled her hair back into a ponytail.

She grabbed Agar's lead and flung open the door.

T-Mac stood there in a pair of shorts and running shoes, nothing else.

All those muscles on his broad, tanned chest sucked the air right out of her lungs.

"Ready?" he asked.

She nodded mutely, exited her quarters with Agar and locked the door behind her.

They took off at a jog, past the rows of containerized living units and out to the open field.

Though she was in good shape and could run several miles without stopping, Kinsley didn't have the long stride of the much-taller SEAL. But she held her own, aware that T-Mac slowed his pace to match hers.

Agar trotted alongside them, happy to be outdoors.

They didn't talk, but ran in companionable silence for a few laps around the open field. When they approached the living quarters again, Kinsley slowed to a walk, breathing hard. "Any clue as to who might have planted that package?"

T-Mac walked beside her, barely having broken a sweat. "None."

"I wish I could remember anything from that night I was shot."

"Don't worry about it," he said. "The guy will surface. And when he does, we'll get him."

"Hopefully before anyone else is hurt." As they reached her unit, she turned. "I'm going to grab my things and hit the shower facility. You can't follow me inside, so don't argue."

"I'll wait outside. But take Agar with you. I'm sure he could use a shower as well."

Kinsley laughed. "I will. He loves the shower."

T-Mac muttered something low, almost indiscernible, but it sounded like *lucky dog*.

Kinsley chose not to read into the comment she might not have even heard correctly. Leaving her door wide open, she entered her unit, grabbed her toiletries kit, towel and clothes, kicked off her running shoes and slipped on her flip-flops. She was outside again in record time.

T-Mac escorted her to the shower facility and waited outside while she and Agar went in. They had the shower to themselves.

Kinsley shampooed Agar first and rinsed him beneath the spray. Then she washed her hair and body, all the while aware of the man right outside the thin walls of the building. As she stood naked under the cool spray, she thought about what it would feel like to share a shower with the SEAL. The man was all muscular and glorious. Would he be disappointed with her pale, freckled body and soft curves? Or would he touch her all over and light her entire body on fire?

Sweet heaven.

Her core heated. The lukewarm water did nothing to tamp down the flames of desire coursing through her veins. Kinsley had to quit thinking about the man and his soft, firm lips, broad shoulders and narrow hips, or she'd melt into a puddle of goo.

Agar stepped out from beneath the spray and shook.

Kinsley rinsed one last time and shut off the shower.

Running the towel over her skin, she dried off briskly, trying not to take too much time. When she was finished, she dressed, brushed her hair back from her forehead and smoothed the tangles free. Agar would dry quickly in the Djibouti heat.

T-Mac was still there when Kinsley stepped out of the shower facility.

He walked her back to her unit and waited for her to enter. "Harm is going to stand guard until I can get showered and changed. But I'll be back for the night."

Kinsley frowned. "You can't sleep in my quarters with me. That would be construed as fraternization."

T-Mac shook his head. "I'm sleeping outside."

"No way. You shouldn't have to sacrifice the comfort of your bed for me."

"I don't consider it a sacrifice. You're doing me a favor. I love to sleep under the stars, and an army cot is what I sleep best on."

"No. This is too much. I can go sleep in the office with whoever is pulling charge of quarters duty. You don't have to babysit me through the night."

He touched her arm. "Anyone ever tell you that you argue too much?"

"Only when I'm right," she replied sharply.

"Well, this time, you aren't going to win the argument. Harm will be here until I return. I'm staying the night outside your unit. The end."

She pressed her lips together. The stubborn set of his jaw brooked no further argument. She'd be talking to a brick wall.

Harm trotted up to stand beside T-Mac. "I'm here." He clapped a hand on T-Mac's shoulder and wrinkled his nose. "Whew, buddy, you smell. Go get your shower."

T-Mac grimaced. "Thanks, Harm."

"I heard from the EOD guys. They said the bomb in the package had a pressure detonator. If she'd stepped on that box, it would have exploded."

T-Mac's gaze went to Kinsley, warming her with the concern in his eyes.

"It's a good thing I have Agar," Kinsley said. "He found it before I would have."

"Maybe I should skip the shower." T-Mac's brow lowered.

"Trust me, dude, you need the shower," Harm said.

T-Mac tipped his head toward Kinsley. "Keep an eye on her."

Harm grinned. "Will do."

"I guess I don't have a say in this?" Kinsley asked, though secretly, she was glad to have such great bodyguards.

Harm glanced at T-Mac.

T-Mac gave a quick head dip. "Nope."

Kinsley rolled her eyes. "Fine. Then keep the noise

down. Agar's a light sleeper." She stepped into her unit and gave Agar the command to follow. Once they were both inside, she closed the door.

Three days ago, she had thought the assignment in Djibouti was going to be boring. Now, with the current threat to her life and the other threat to her heart…Djibouti was anything but boring.

T-MAC HATED BEING even a minute away from Kinsley. He couldn't be certain whoever had planted the package bomb wouldn't try again, or when.

He made it to his quarters and back to the shower facility in record time. He scrubbed clean and shaved, wishing he had time to get a haircut. But he'd already been gone more than eight minutes.

Back at his quarters, he grabbed a folding cot and returned to Kinsley's building.

Harm leaned against the corner of the unit. When he spotted T-Mac, he straightened. "What took you so long?" Then he chuckled. "Just kidding. Did you even wash behind your ears? That was faster than a shower at BUD/S training."

T-Mac clapped a hand onto Harm's shoulder. "Didn't want you to suffer for too long."

"Suffer? Or you didn't want me to tell your dog handler all your faults?"

"Both," T-Mac said.

Harm moved closer. "Big Jake hobbled by while you were AWOL from your post."

"And?" T-Mac prompted.

His friend glanced around and lowered his voice. "He was at the command center."

T-Mac drew in a breath and let it out slowly. "Are we a go?"

"Soon." He looked over his shoulder at the door to Kinsley's unit. "Are you ready?"

"I am."

Harm tipped his head toward the door. "Are you ready for her?"

"For Specialist Anderson to come along?" T-Mac sighed. "I don't have much choice, do I?" He shrugged. "I guess I am. Any idea when?"

With a shake of his head, Harm squared his shoulders. "Nope. Just be ready."

Which meant no sleep.

Harm left T-Mac alone.

He set up his cot in front of Kinsley's unit. A few people walked by, giving him strange looks, but he ignored them and stretched out with his hands locked behind his head. If he slept, it would be just a catnap, with one eye open. Darkness had settled in on Camp Lemonnier and the stars popped out, a few at a time, soon making enough light that he didn't need a flashlight to see.

The beauty of the night sky, filled with an array of diamond-like stars, made up for the daylight drabness of the desert surroundings.

A soft click sounded behind him.

He turned as the door to Kinsley's unit opened.

Agar trotted out.

Kinsley stood in the crack and gave Agar the command to lie down.

Agar dropped to his belly on the ground beside T-Mac's cot.

Before he could tell Kinsley that he didn't need Agar's protection, she closed the door.

Agar lifted his head beside the cot. T-Mac reached over and smoothed his hand over the dog's back. "She has a mind of her own, doesn't she?"

When T-Mac's hand stopped moving, Agar nuzzled his fingers.

"Needy guy, aren't you?" T-Mac scratched behind Agar's ears and rubbed his back again. He'd rather be running his hands over Kinsley's naked body than over her dog's back, but this was safer.

He must have drifted off, because the next moment, he awakened to the low rumble of Agar's growl.

T-Mac popped to a sitting position, his fist clenched, ready to defend.

A dark figure disengaged from the shadow of one of the container units.

"T-Mac," Harm's voice called to him in a half whisper.

"Yeah."

"It's time."

Chapter Eight

A finger pressed to her lips and a voice sounded in the darkness. "Kinsley, wake up."

Immediately, Kinsley knocked the hand away, and she shot to a sitting position. "What the hell?"

"I knocked lightly, but you didn't answer. I couldn't knock louder without waking others."

She pushed the hair out of her face and stared up at T-Mac. "It's okay. You just startled me."

"You left your door unlocked."

Agar nudged her fingers with his cool, damp nose.

Kinsley smoothed a hand over his head and neck. "I know. With you out there, I wasn't worried someone would break in."

"What if someone slit my throat?"

She yawned and stretched. "Agar wouldn't let that happen." The room seemed smaller with T-Mac in it. "Why did you wake me?" Her eyes widened. "Oh. Is it time?"

He nodded. "Get your gear. Harm's outside. I'll be back in less than five minutes to get you."

She nodded.

He turned toward the door. "Oh, and did you know you snore?"

"No, I do not." She frowned. "Do I?"

He grinned. "You do. And it's cute as hell. Don't let anyone tell you otherwise." He left her sitting on her bunk with her mouth open.

As soon as he shut the door, she was off the bed and dressing in her uniform, body armor loaded with ammunition and a first-aid kit. She pulled on her helmet, grabbed her rifle and snapped Agar's retractable lead onto his collar. By the time she was ready, a soft knock sounded on the door. She opened it to find T-Mac standing on the other side.

Without a word, she stepped out with Agar, closed the door softly behind her and locked it.

They hurried toward the helicopters on the flight line where the rest of the SEAL team had assembled. Already the rotor blades were turning. If someone didn't know they were about to go on a mission before, they knew now.

The SEAL team loaded into the helicopters. Agar jumped in, and T-Mac gave Kinsley a hand up. Even before she had her safety harness buckled, the chopper left the ground and rose into the air.

Kinsley settled back in her seat and willed her pulse to slow. Agar sat between her legs, his chin on her lap. She stroked his fur, calming him as well as herself. The mission seemed to be happening so fast. The silence made it seem all the more dangerous.

She could imagine what it would be like to be one of them on a mission without her and the dog. They probably moved like a well-oiled machine. Each had a position or a part to play, and they did it well. Perhaps T-Mac had been right in concluding she was a distraction. She didn't belong in this group of highly trained fighters.

Sure, she was a good shot and knew basic fighting tactics, but she wasn't like them. They were finely honed weapons in and of themselves.

Then again, the SEALs weren't like Agar. The dog would help to protect them when they couldn't sniff out danger lurking beneath their feet.

She tried not to be so completely aware of T-Mac's thigh pressed against hers. She couldn't move away from him, since they were packed tightly together and Agar gave her no room to shift her legs.

The heat from T-Mac's thigh scorched her own, sending electrical currents through her leg and straight to her core, making her burn with sexy images of him in his PT shorts and bare chest. Her fingers tingled, itching to touch him, to run her hands over his taut muscles and down to… Sweet heaven, how could she even think naughty thoughts of the man when they could be descending into yet another hotbed of enemy activity?

Her mind should be on the task ahead, not the man beside her. She should be planning her and Agar's next moves. But T-Mac was right there beside her, tempting her like no other man ever had.

"FAST FIVE" READER SURVEY

Your participation entitles you to:
✴ **4 Thank-You Gifts Worth Over $20!**

Complete the survey in minutes.

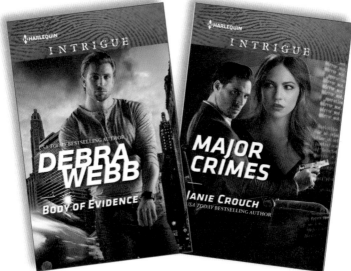

Get **2 FREE** Books

Your Thank-You Gifts include **2 FREE BOOKS** and **2 MYSTERY GIFTS**. There's no obligation to purchase anything!

See inside for details.

Please help make our
"Fast Five" Reader Survey
a success!

Dear Reader,

Since you are a lover of our books, your opinions are important to us... and so is your time.

That's why we made sure your **"FAST FIVE" READER SURVEY** can be completed in just a few minutes. Your answers to the five questions will help us remain at the forefront of women's fiction.

And, as a thank-you for participating, we'd like to send you **4 FREE THANK-YOU GIFTS!**

Enjoy your gifts with our appreciation,

Pam Powers

To get your
4 FREE THANK-YOU GIFTS:

✴ Quickly complete the "Fast Five" Reader Survey
and return the insert.

"FAST FIVE" READER SURVEY

1 Do you sometimes read a book a second or third time? ○ Yes ○ No

2 Do you often choose reading over other forms of entertainment such as television? ○ Yes ○ No

3 When you were a child, did someone regularly read aloud to you? ○ Yes ○ No

4 Do you sometimes take a book with you when you travel outside the home? ○ Yes ○ No

5 In addition to books, do you regularly read newspapers and magazines? ○ Yes ○ No

YES! I have completed the above Reader Survey. Please send me my 4 FREE GIFTS (gifts worth over $20 retail). I understand that I am under no obligation to buy anything, as explained on the back of this card.

❏ I prefer the regular-print edition
182/382 HDL GM34

❏ I prefer the larger-print edition
199/399 HDL GM34

FIRST NAME	LAST NAME

ADDRESS

APT.#	CITY

STATE/PROV.	ZIP/POSTAL CODE

READER SERVICE—Here's how it works:

▲ If offer card is missing write to: Reader Service, P.O. Box 1341, Buffalo, NY 14240-8531 or visit www.ReaderService.com ▲

BUSINESS REPLY MAIL
FIRST-CLASS MAIL   PERMIT NO. 717   BUFFALO, NY

POSTAGE WILL BE PAID BY ADDRESSEE

READER SERVICE
PO BOX 1341
BUFFALO NY 14240-8571

NO POSTAGE
NECESSARY
IF MAILED
IN THE
UNITED STATES

After half an hour in the air, she'd settled back in her seat and tried to relax, determined to conserve her energy for whatever lay in store for her next. But she was too wound up, thinking about the last time she'd gone out on a mission. Her heart pounded in her chest and her ribs were still sore from the impact of the bullet on her armored vest. At her current pulse rate, she'd be worn out before they landed. She let her hand fall to her side between her and T-Mac.

A moment later, T-Mac's fingers curled around hers, hidden between them from anyone else's view.

His touch at once calmed her and excited her for an entirely different reason. She didn't question it, just drew on his strength.

By the time they landed, she had pulled herself together, ready to face whatever fate had in store for her and Agar.

As soon as the helicopters landed, the SEALs leaped to the ground. Agar was quick to exit, and Kinsley jumped down beside him.

T-Mac was there with a hand on her elbow to steady her until she had her balance.

As soon as they were all on the ground, the helicopters lifted into the air and headed back the way they'd come. The crew would wait within radio distance for the call to extract the team.

Kinsley couldn't help but feel a little stranded as she watched the choppers disappear into the night. She hefted her rifle in one hand and gripped Agar's lead in the other.

"Comm check," Big Jake said.

Kinsley worried that his slight limp would slow him down. But the big guy seemed as determined as the rest to find the people responsible for the attack on them in the last operation that had gone south.

One by one, all six of the SEALs checked in with only their call signs.

Once all of the SEALs had called out their names, T-Mac nudged Kinsley.

"Dog handler and Agar," Kinsley added to the tail end of the comm check. She could hear her voice in the radio and was reassured by the sound. If nothing else, she was connected by radio. If she got separated from the others, she could still connect this way.

"Let's do this," Big Jake said.

T-Mac touched Kinsley's shoulder and nodded in the direction they were heading.

"I'm right next to you," he said into his mic. "We have a lot of ground to cover between us and our target."

Kinsley warmed at his voice coming through the radio in her ear. With T-Mac at her side, she didn't have to worry if she was going the right way. While she concentrated on Agar, T-Mac would make sure they were on track.

Giving Agar the command to search, she followed the dog, moving out quickly. If they wanted to get there in a hurry, Agar had to work his magic without interruption.

As before, the dog sailed past the first mile without stopping.

The second mile, they traversed over rougher terrain, heading into hills with lots of scrub trees and bushes blocking their view ahead.

Agar kept his nose to the ground, working his way back and forth across the path.

Kinsley never let her guard down, constantly watching for any sign from the animal that things weren't all they should be.

"We're getting close to the target coordinates," T-Mac warned. "Slow the dog."

Kinsley pulled back on Agar's lead, checking his progress. The dog immediately returned to her side and looked up at her, his tongue lolling.

She would like to have given him some of the water she carried in her CamelBak thermos, but they didn't have time to stop. Keeping Agar on a shorter lead this time, she sent him forward to sniff for explosives.

"Half a click," T-Mac whispered. "Be on the lookout for guards on the perimeter."

"Roger," Big Jake answered. "You, too."

Ten steps later, Agar lay down.

Kinsley stuck a flag in the ground where he lay and moved on. Five flags later, Agar was moving faster again.

She gave him more of a lead, allowing him to swing wider from center. When he didn't come up with anything, he raced back in the opposite direction, clearing a wider path.

Kinsley understood the need to move slowly, but she also knew the element of surprise could require striking swiftly. The SEALs liked to get in and get the job done.

But she focused on her work with Agar, determined to deliver the team safely to the coordinates. That was her and Agar's primary responsibility. If they didn't accomplish that, what was the purpose of including them on the mission?

T-Mac grabbed her arm and pulled her to the ground. "Tango at two o'clock." He held up his fist for the guys behind him, indicating they should stop in place.

Agar was as far out as his retractable lead would go, still sniffing out bombs and land mines.

Kinsley couldn't call him back without alerting the man pulling guard duty on the perimeter. She tugged the lead.

Instead of coming, as he usually did, he braced his paws in the dirt and strained against his lead.

Kinsley tugged again. Resisting a touch command was not like Agar. The dog always came when he was called or tugged.

"Why is he just standing there?" T-Mac asked.

"Something or someone is out there, not too far from where Agar is standing." Her heart pounding, Kinsley remained in position with one knee on the ground. She aimed her rifle in front of her, ready to take down anyone who tried to attack the team or Agar.

"I'm going forward," T-Mac said.

Kinsley wanted to hold him back, but knew she couldn't. Agar had cleared the path between them, but not beyond. All she could hope was that there were no more land mines or other explosives between Agar and the Tango crouched out of sight beyond.

When T-Mac moved past Agar, Kinsley tugged hard on his lead, calling the dog back to her side.

This time Agar complied, as if he knew he'd done his job and T-Mac would take it from there.

Kinsley held her breath, praying no explosives lay in T-Mac's path. She squatted low to the ground, her hand on Agar's back, her heart pounding an erratic tattoo against her ribs.

T-Mac moved from bush to tree, clinging to the shadows cast by the starlight. Before long, even Kinsley couldn't make him out against the gloom of darkness. The man was like a cat moving through the night after his prey.

A movement beside her made Agar growl low in his chest.

Harm dropped to his knee at her side. "Do you see him?" he asked quietly into her headset.

"No," she responded. "I lost him."

"He's almost to the guy." Harm pointed into the darkness. "Let's hope the guard is asleep."

Kinsley nodded, never taking her gaze from the last place she'd seen T-Mac.

"One down," T-Mac whispered into her headset.

Then a shadow leaped up from a different location and ran away from the team.

"Got a live one on the loose," Harm called out softly.

"Hold your fire. We can't alert the rest of the camp until we can no longer avoid it," Big Jake warned.

"But he's going to alert the others," T-Mac said.

"Not if I can help it." Kinsley unclipped the lead from Agar's collar and gave him the command to take down.

Agar leaped forward and chased after the running man. Within seconds, he hit the man in the back, knocking him to his knees.

The SEAL team closed in.

Kinsley ran to catch up to Agar.

But before she could reach him, a shot rang out.

Shouts sounded ahead and lights flared out of the darkness. Half a dozen pairs of headlights came to life, chasing away the darkness and ruining any night vision they could have hoped for.

"Get down," Big Jake spoke sharply into the headset.

Kinsley didn't have to be told twice. She dropped to her knees, then down to a prone position, her rifle in her hand, aimed at the headlights, waiting for movement.

"Things are about to go sideways," Big Jake said. "Take out who you need to—save a live one to bring back."

Shouts sounded from the camp and gunfire echoed in the sky.

The men moved forward, slipping into the shadows now cast by the many vehicle headlights glowing.

Kinsley eased her way toward Agar and the man whose arm he held between his razor-sharp teeth.

Harm had been there a moment before, dispatching the man with a clean swipe across the neck with his wicked Ka-Bar knife.

Kinsley shuddered and gave Agar the command to release. Agar shook the dead man once more and then let go of his arm and returned to Kinsley's side.

Harm moved on, leaving Kinsley and Agar alone with the dead man.

As Kinsley moved past the man on the ground, he reached out and grabbed her ankle.

Kinsley screamed and dropped to the ground, kicking at the hand.

Agar leaped to her defense, sinking his teeth into the man's arm.

Kicking wouldn't release the man's grip. She reached down and peeled back the fingers on the hand, finally freeing her ankle.

"Kinsley, are you all right?" T-Mac's voice sounded in her ears.

"I'm okay," she said.

"Where are you?" he demanded.

"I don't know," she admitted. "Not far from where you left me, I think."

All the SEALs had converged on the camp.

"Stay put—I'll find you."

Moments later, T-Mac appeared in front of her.

Kinsley leaped to her feet and fell into his arms.

More headlights flashed from another direction, heading toward the position where Kinsley, Agar and T-Mac stood.

"Come on. We have to get out of here." T-Mac took her hand.

Together they ran around the perimeter, away from the vehicles heading into the camp.

At one point, T-Mac pulled her down to a crouch.

He glanced back in the direction from which they'd come. For a moment, he remained silent. Then he spoke into his headset. "Gang, you need to get out of there. Four trucks loaded with at least ten men each, all armed, are on their way in. You're about to be grossly outnumbered."

"Calling for extraction." Big Jake's voice came over the radio. "Meet at the alternate pickup point, ASAP."

"Where's the alternate pickup point?" Kinsley asked.

"Two kilometers north of our original drop zone."

"Aren't we—"

"South of the camp and our pickup location?" T-Mac grunted. "Yes."

"And aren't those trucks filled with all those re-inforcements standing between us and our ride back to Camp Lemonnier?"

"Give the girl a prize." He touched her shoulder. "We'll be okay."

"We have a man down," Harm called out. "We've got him, but we're moving slowly toward the pickup point. Someone cover our backs."

"Gotcha covered," Diesel said. "Go!"

"Getting hot in here," Buck reported. "Heading out. Don't shoot me."

"Those trucks are less than a kilometer away," T-Mac reminded him. "If you're getting out, now would be a good time."

"What about you?" Big Jake asked. "Give me a sitrep, T-Mac."

"We're between a rock and a hard place. Get the injured back to the Lemon. The dog handler and I will stay low until you can send reinforcements back to collect us."

"We're not leaving without you," Big Jake said.

"You can't delay getting that man some medical attention. We'll be all right."

The chatter stilled.

Kinsley held her breath, her heart pounding. "Are we staying?" she asked.

"Looks like it," T-Mac answered. "We can't delay the choppers from getting the men back to Camp Lemonnier."

"Okay." She was with T-Mac. He'd promised to keep her safe. She trusted he would keep that promise. Kinsley sucked in a deep breath and let it out. "What now?"

T-Mac didn't like that he and Kinsley were trapped more or less behind enemy lines. He had to get her safely away from the terrorist camp and hunker down somewhere safe and out of sight until the helicopters could return to pick them up.

His night-vision goggles were useless with all the headlights lighting up the sky. But as long as they weren't pointed directly at them, they could move without being obvious. If their night vision was compromised, so too would the terrorists'.

He checked his compass using a red-lensed flashlight and nodded in the direction they should travel to get away from the commotion. "Let's go."

"Wait." Kinsley touched his arm. "Let Agar go ahead of us."

"We don't have time."

"And we don't have time to be blown up. You saw the mines were set out between one and two kilometers outside the camp. If they set them out on all sides, let Agar find them for us."

"Okay, but we have to move fast. Right now they're probably concerned about the larger group of SEALs. When they're gone, they'll have time to look for others. That would be us. We can't let them see us, or our ducks are cooked."

Kinsley laughed. "Ducks are cooked?"

T-Mac liked the sound of her laughter, even if it was only nerves. "You know what I mean."

"I do, but ducks?" She laughed again but fell in step, moving hunched over.

They crouched as low as possible to the ground to keep from being seen or captured in the light from a moving vehicle.

Agar searched ahead, his nose to the ground, a silent shadow moving back and forth at the end of his lead.

So far, he hadn't found anything, but that didn't mean he wouldn't.

A loud explosion sounded from the other side of the camp. T-Mac's heart plummeted.

"Oh, no," Kinsley said softly.

"One of our guys stepped on a land mine," Buck reported over the radio headset. "He's in a bad way. Really bad."

T-Mac stopped and cursed. He hovered between getting farther away and heading back to help his team. But he had an obligation to protect Kinsley. If he took her with him to help his teammates, she'd be in danger and might either be shot or captured.

"We have to go back," Kinsley said.

Her words brought him back to reality. Even if he could get past the four truckloads of men entering camp, he couldn't drag Kinsley into the middle of the mayhem.

"We can't go back." His jaw hardened. "My team will return to collect us after they get the injured to safety."

"But Agar could have gotten them out without un-necessary injuries."

"SEAL teams don't usually have the benefit of a Military Working Dog looking out for us. However, we wouldn't have made it as far as we have tonight without you and Agar."

"I wish we could have kept that SEAL from step-ping on the explosives."

"We can't second-guess our decisions. Right now we have to lie low and hope we aren't discovered." He kept moving, farther and farther away from the terrorist compound until they could barely see the individual headlights. All they could discern were lights shining out from the camp center.

"How does your team know where to pick you up if you get separated?"

"I'm carrying a GPS tracking device. And when they get close enough, we'll reestablish radio com-munication with our headsets."

"In the meantime, shouldn't we conserve the bat-tery on these?" She pointed to the device in her ear.

"Yes." He pulled his radio headset off and stuffed it into one of the pockets on his uniform.

Kinsley did the same. "Are we stopping for a few minutes?" she asked.

"We can." T-Mac pulled his night-vision goggles down and glanced around the area, careful not to look directly at the terrorist camp with its bright headlights still burning. He didn't see the green heat signatures of people moving about in the area, and they were far enough away that they couldn't see them. He raised the NVGs and nodded. "Rest for a few minutes."

"Good. Agar needs water." She looped her weapon strap over her shoulder, cupped her hand and squirted water into her palm from the CamelBak water-storage device she wore like a backpack over her body armor.

Agar eagerly lapped up the water and waited while she repeated the process several times until he was satisfied. Then he lay on the ground beside her, seemingly content to rest as long as she was still.

"How long do you think it will take them to come back for us?" she whispered.

"I'm not sure. But it would be good for us to get as far away from the compound as we can before they attempt to bring the helicopter back. Now that the terrorists know we know where they are, they will be moving. And we don't know which direction they will go."

"They could be heading this way?" Kinsley rubbed her hands up and down her arms. "We are south of them, right?"

"Right."

"Wouldn't it be better if someone knew where they were headed?" she asked.

T-Mac didn't like the question, or the direction of her thoughts. "What do you have in mind?"

"If you have a GPS device on you, couldn't you attach it to one of their vehicles? That way we wouldn't have to rely on satellite images to find them again."

"But then our guys would have no way of finding us. And believe me, it's a long way back to Camp Lemonnier on foot."

Kinsley stared at the ground beside Agar and ran her hand over his head. "It's a shame. These terrorists will probably be gone by morning."

"Military intelligence could pull more satellite photos. They'll find them again."

"You heard the commander. The intel guys said it was lucky they actually found them the first time." She shook her head. "Those bastards could get away again. They'll only go on to hurt more of our military personnel, not to mention the innocent people they terrorize on a daily basis."

"It's too bad we don't have one of the vehicles we saw tonight," Kinsley mused. "We could plant the GPS device and make our way back to Camp Lemonnier on our own."

"To do that, we'd have to steal one of their vehicles," T-Mac said. "It would be insane to try." Then why the hell was he considering trying to steal one of the trucks he'd seen that evening?

But the more he thought about it, the more he liked the idea. He could do it. But would he put Kinsley at too much risk by even attempting such an idiotic feat?

He glanced down at where Kinsley sat beside

Agar. "I know you're good at finding land mines and IEDs, but how are you with setting detonators in plastic explosives?"

Chapter Nine

After a quick refresher on detonators and C-4 explosives, Kinsley worked with T-Mac to divvy up what he'd come with into three separate setups.

The camp would still be in a state of disarray, with everyone loading up whatever they deemed valuable in preparation for bugging out. They wouldn't want to stay in one place knowing their location was compromised. After the Navy SEAL attack, they would be expecting even more grief in the way of rockets launched by either UAVs or other military aircraft. If they didn't get out that night, they would be easy targets.

"Since we haven't seen guards out searching for anyone left behind, we can assume they think all of the personnel who participated in the attack are gone for now," T-Mac said. "We have surprise on our side. They will not be expecting anyone else to launch an offensive anytime soon."

Kinsley squared her shoulders, excitement building in her chest. "That's where we come in."

Even in the limited lighting from the stars overhead, she could see the way T-Mac's brow dipped. "Not *we*," he said. "*I* will set the charges in strategic locations."

"Right," she agreed. "While Agar and I hide nearby."

"Exactly." T-Mac continued. "Then, while the Al-Shabaab terrorists are confused by the explosions, I'll see what I can appropriate in the way of a vehicle. You'll need to be ready once I roll out of the camp."

She nodded, wishing she could play a bigger role in the attack. "Agar and I will be ready."

T-Mac pressed a button on the side of his watch. "They should be scrambling out of the camp soon. If we're going, we should leave now and get as close as possible without being seen." He nodded toward Agar. "Will you be able to keep him quiet while I'm setting the charges?"

"Absolutely," she replied, confident in Agar's ability to take command.

"Then let's go." Together, they loaded the detonators into pouches and secured them on his vest. Then they loaded the C-4 into another pouch and secured the pouch to his vest. In order to move quickly, he would leave his rifle with Kinsley and carry only his handgun, Ka-Bar knife and a couple of hand grenades.

Now that they were actually going back to the camp, Kinsley was positive her idea was insane. But no matter how much she wanted to change T-Mac's mind, he was set on his course.

Once he had everything where he could reach it quickly, he stared down at Kinsley. "You can stay here, if you like. I could make it back to you in whatever vehicle I can commandeer, or if that's not possible, I can return on foot and we'll get the hell out of here."

"I'm coming as close as I can get. If you run into difficulties, I can cover for you while you get out."

He shook his head. "I don't know. The more I think about it, the more I'm convinced you'd be better off staying here."

"I'm not staying. You can't go it completely alone. You might get in okay, but getting back out will be more difficult. They'll be looking for whoever set off the explosions." She touched his arm, ready to do what it took to convince him she was an asset, not a liability. "I'm a pretty decent shot. I qualify expert every time I've been to the range. The least I can do is provide cover for you."

"Being that close to camp puts you at risk."

"I signed up for this gig when I asked to train with the dogs. I knew we'd be on the front line at some point. I'd say this is pretty damn close to the front line." She lifted her chin. "I'm not afraid."

"You might not be afraid for yourself." He cupped her cheek in his palm. "But I'm scared for you." He tipped his head toward the dog. "And Agar."

Her heart warmed at the concern in his voice. She

leaned her cheek into his palm. "Don't worry about us. I'll stay low and still. They won't even know I'm there. You just do your thing and create the biggest, loudest distraction you can. I'll be waiting near the road they drove in on. It should be clear of all land mines or they wouldn't have driven in from that direction."

"And you'll have Agar if you get into trouble." He stared down into her face.

T-Mac's eyes were inky pools in the starlight, and Kinsley couldn't read into them. By the way he leaned toward her, she could sense he wanted to say or do more. When he hesitated, she made up his mind for him and leaned up on her toes, pressing her lips to his. "Be careful, will ya? I kind of like kissing you."

He laughed. "You know we could be court-martialed for fraternizing."

She shrugged. "And we might not live to see the dawn of a new day. I'll take my chances." And she kissed him again.

T-Mac gripped her shoulders and pulled her into his embrace, their body armor making it difficult to get closer. "This doesn't end here," he promised.

"I'm banking on that, frogman." She squared her shoulders. "Let's do this."

Though she was scared, adrenaline kicked in and sent her forward. She gave Agar the command to search ahead of them. While he sniffed for explosives in the ground, Kinsley looked at the activity going on in the terrorist camp. They appeared to be loading trucks. Men moved in front of headlights, carrying boxes and other items.

If T-Mac didn't hurry, he might miss the opportunity to tag one of the vehicles and claim one of them for their own.

Kinsley couldn't make Agar move faster. He was doing his job, but apparently between them and the camp there were no land mines. The terrorists must have thought the threats wouldn't come from the south, deeper into Somalia.

Within minutes, they were back in shooting range of the camp.

Kinsley's heart beat faster and her level of fear intensified. She didn't like the idea of T-Mac slipping back into camp to set explosive charges. She couldn't even imagine if he got caught. She prayed it wouldn't happen, that he'd make it in and back out unscathed.

Just outside the camp, close to the road T-Mac was due to escape on, they hunkered low in the brush.

Kinsley sought out T-Mac's hand, having massive second thoughts. "Don't worry about swiping a vehicle. Just get in, plant the GPS and get back out. We'll find our way back to Camp Lemonnier on foot. In fact, let's not do this at all. I'd rather not lose you at this point."

He squeezed her hand and brought it to his lips. "I'll be fine. But thanks for caring." He kissed the backs of her knuckles. "Remember, I'll be driving with the lights out. I'll give three beams of my flashlight in quick succession."

Kinsley smiled. "And I'll return it with a beam from my red-lensed flashlight."

"We might have to repeat the cue a couple of times if I'm off on distance."

"I'll be watching." She sighed and stared up into his eyes. "Hurry back. I'm kinda getting used to having you around, big guy." Kinsley cupped his cheek. "And don't do anything stupid."

"Stupid isn't in the repertoire of a SEAL," he said. "Hang tight. This shouldn't take too long." He kissed her hard on the lips and took off.

Agar strained at the lead, eager to follow, but Kinsley held firm. For the first few minutes, she could follow T-Mac's silhouette moving through the brush and past trees, working his way toward the vehicles and people milling around the camp. Once he reached one of the tents still standing, he disappeared.

Kinsley's heart lodged in her throat and her pulse pounded so hard, she could barely hear herself think.

Minutes ticked by like hours.

If he didn't come out, she and Agar were on their own to make it back to Camp Lemonnier. But that didn't scare her as badly as the fact that if he didn't make it out, it meant he was either dead or captured and would be tortured by the terrorists.

Kinsley didn't know which would be worse. But she knew one thing... She was falling for the navy SEAL, and she didn't want what she felt for him to end like this.

MAKING IT INTO the camp hadn't been that difficult. The terrorists were in a frenetic hurry to break camp, pack the trucks and get the hell out before their attackers returned with mortars or missiles.

T-Mac hid in the shadow of a tent, studying the layout of the camp, determining where would be the best place to set his charges. To make the biggest bang for his effort, he'd have to take out a couple of the trucks. The pile of empty crates at the north end of the camp would be a good target, drawing attention to the north while T-Mac attempted to take a vehicle and head south, as if one of the terrorists had gotten a jump start on leaving the compound.

Once his decision was made, he went into action, stealing from shadow to shadow. Men in black robes and turbans raced past him, their weapons slung over their shoulders, each carrying something to load into the backs of trucks.

T-Mac slipped up behind one at the back of a lone truck at the north end of the compound, grabbed him from behind and snapped his neck, killing him instantly. He dragged him under the truck, stripped off his turban and robe and dressed in them. He'd have a better chance of mixing in with the bad guys dressed like them.

Then he planted the plastic explosives near the engine of the vehicle and pressed a detonator into the claylike material. Lifting a small crate, he ran through the camp like the others until he arrived at another vehicle on the northwest side and stood behind another man loading a box into the back. He handed his crate up to the man in the back of the truck and turned to leave.

The man in the truck shouted something to him.

T-Mac didn't catch what he said, so he couldn't translate. He pretended he didn't hear and hurried toward the front of the truck, where he pressed another glob of plastic explosives into the metal and jammed a detonator into it.

Once he had the two trucks tagged with explosives, he hurried toward several barrels that he assumed contained fuel of some sort. As he walked with his hands under the robe, he pressed another detonator into the C-4. Once he reached the barrels, he mashed the explosive compound into the side of one of the barrels that felt full.

A shout from behind made him turn.

Fortunately, the man wasn't shouting at him, but at another man who'd dropped a container full of boxes of ammunition, spilling its contents over the ground. Bullets spilled out and rolled across the sand.

A couple of the men ganged up on the one who'd dropped the box.

While all attention was on them, T-Mac slipped to the south side of the camp, eyeing two vehicles already pointed toward Somalia. Men were loading boxes and weapons into the backs of the trucks. On the one closest to him, a driver sat in the cab, his weapon resting across his lap.

T-Mac hoped the fireworks would distract all of

them long enough for him to get the truck and get the hell out of camp before anyone knew any better.

He found a position behind the hulk of a vehicle that had flat tires and had been stripped of anything that could be removed, cannibalized or destroyed. Once he was safely in place, he covered his ears, hunkered down and pressed the button to detonate the first charge.

The explosion shook the ground beneath him.

Screams and shouts rose up around him.

From the corner of his hiding place, he watched as half of the men who'd been loading his target truck and the one beside it ran toward the explosion.

Five seconds later, he set off round two.

Again, the explosion made the earth tremble beneath his feet and debris rain down from the sky.

Daring to peek out, T-Mac checked the truck he hoped to steal. The driver had stepped down from the cab, his weapon raised, his gaze darting around, apparently searching for the person setting off the charges. Yet he didn't move away from the vehicle.

T-Mac would have to take the guy down.

He gauged how far he'd have to run out in the open to get to the driver, knowing he could easily do it, especially since he was disguised as one of them.

Gunfire sounded as the terrorists ran to the north end of the compound.

Knowing it was his last chance to create a huge distraction, T-Mac waited a few seconds before detonating the last charge.

Boom! The charge went off. A second later, another, louder bang ripped through the night, sending a tower of flames into the air as the fuel in the barrel ignited.

The truck driver hit the ground and covered his head.

T-Mac made his move. He sprinted across the open space, bent to the man on the ground and slit his throat. With the driver out of the way and the others all concentrating on the north end of camp and the raging fire sending flames a hundred feet into the sky, T-Mac had the chance he'd been hoping for.

He dragged the man beneath the truck, ran to the other vehicle and stashed the GPS tracker in a ripped hole in the driver's seat. Once he had the reason for his visit to the camp in place, he ran back around the front of the truck he hoped to take, leaned into the cab, set it in Neutral and started pushing it toward the perimeter of the camp.

At first, the truck barely moved. But once he got the momentum going, it rolled faster and faster. When he reached the edge of the camp, he jumped into the cab, twisted the key in the ignition and cranked the engine.

A shout sounded beside the driver's door. A man in the black garb of the Al-Shabaab ran alongside the truck, shaking his fist at T-Mac.

T-Mac slowed enough to position the vehicle just right, then shoved the door open fast and hard, hitting the man in the head.

The guy fell to the ground and lay still.

T-Mac didn't wait around to see if he revived. He didn't have time. As soon as the excitement of the explosions waned, the men in the camp would notice one of their vehicles had disappeared and some of their men were down. Someone else might have seen the truck leaving camp and the direction it had gone. T-Mac had to find Kinsley fast and get as far away from the terrorists as they could.

Once outside the camp, he pressed the accelerator to the floor, sending the truck leaping forward. He couldn't go far at that speed or he'd be forced to use the brakes without knowing if the brake lights would light up.

When he got to within range of where he'd left Kinsley, he pulled out his flashlight and hit the on-off switch three times. He scanned the darkness, praying for a red light blinking back at him.

For the longest moments of his life, he waited. When he didn't see anything, he repeated the three bursts of light.

Damn, had he gone out in the wrong direction? Had she been discovered and captured? Where was she? If he didn't find her soon, he wasn't sure they'd make it out of there undiscovered. He searched the darkness, desperately looking for the silhouette of a woman and a dog, praying they were all right.

Just when he considered turning back, a red dot appeared in the darkness.

Chapter Ten

Kinsley hated waiting, not knowing what was happening. The first twenty minutes were hell, with every possible bad scenario rolling through her mind.

With all the terrorists running around the camp, how could T-Mac get in and do the job without being seen? The operation wasn't like one where they sneaked in while everyone was sleeping. He was going into a stirred-up hornets' nest to stir it up even more.

The more she sat waiting, the more she convinced herself this mission was a very bad idea.

When the first explosion went off, she jumped. She felt an immediate mixture of relief and even more tension.

T-Mac had managed to get in and set at least one charge.

Agar whined softly beside her, but stayed in his prone position, head down, resting. He could be up and running at her command.

The second explosion went off. The corners of Kinsley's lips quirked upward. Two down, one to go.

"Come on, T-Mac," she whispered softly.

At the third explosion, she wanted to cheer, but the ensuing fireball rising into the air made her heart drop into her belly.

Had something gone wrong? Had T-Mac been caught up in whatever caused the fireball?

Her heart pounded so hard, her pulse beat against her eardrums, making it hard for her to hear.

Men ran around the camp, shouting, their bodies black silhouettes against the bright orange blaze of what Kinsley suspected was burning fuel.

She didn't care how T-Mac got out of the camp as long as he got out alive. If he didn't find a way to commandeer a vehicle, they'd figure out a way to get back to Camp Lemonnier on foot.

He just needed to hurry.

The giant flame held Kinsley's attention, destroying her night vision. She didn't see the truck racing toward her until it was close enough she could hear the engine.

She prayed T-Mac was driving. What had he said? He'd give her three flashes from his flashlight?

Kinsley held her breath, waiting as the dark hulk of the truck grew closer.

Then a bright white light shone out from the cab.

Her pulse sped and she laughed out loud. "It's him, Agar!" she cried.

Agar jumped up, jerking the lead right out of her hand.

Afraid the dog would run out in front of the truck, Kinsley gave him the command to sit.

Agar sat.

Kinsley patted the ground, searching for the lead. When she found it, she looked up again.

The truck was much closer, moving slowly but almost to where she lay waiting in the brush. Another three flashes of light blinked into the night.

Oh, no.

Kinsley fumbled to unclip her flashlight from her web gear. She was supposed to flash her red-lensed flashlight back to indicate where she was. If she didn't hurry, he'd pass her. Then she'd be left behind. T-Mac couldn't shine his bright beam back toward the camp without alerting the terrorists to their location.

Her hand trembled as she pressed the switch. Nothing happened. Damn. Now wasn't the time for an equipment malfunction.

She slapped the device against her palm and the red light came on. Quickly, she held it up, aiming the red orb at the oncoming truck.

She heard the engine throttle down as if being placed into low gear. It slowed, rolling past her so slowly, she jumped up and ran after it, Agar trotting alongside her.

The screech of an emergency brake sounded, and the truck stopped with a jerk.

T-Mac dropped down from the cab, ran back to

her and wrapped her in his arms. "I thought I'd come out of the camp on the wrong road."

"I thought you'd never get here." She laughed and stood on her toes to press a kiss to his lips. "Let's get out of here."

"Good idea." He held the driver's-side door.

Agar leaped up into the cab.

Kinsley climbed in and scooted over.

T-Mac hopped in, shifted into gear and took off as fast as he could without headlights to guide them. Thankfully, the stars shone bright enough to light their way.

With Agar in the passenger seat, Kinsley sat in the middle, her thigh pressed against T-Mac's, the reassuring strength of him warming her all the way through. She could breathe again.

"GPS?" she quizzed as she removed her helmet.

"Planted," he shot back.

"Thank God." Kinsley settled back in her seat, hesitant to pull off her armored vest so soon. "How far south are we going?"

"Not very." He glanced sideways at her. "We need to find a place to hide and wait for Al-Shabaab to move past, however long that takes."

"Aren't you worried we'll run into more of them coming up from the south to see what the fire is all about?"

"A little. The sooner we find a place to hide, the better."

Kinsley stared out into the darkness, focusing on

anything large enough to hide a truck behind. For the first few miles, the land was flat and dry. Only a few bushes and scrubby trees stood out against the desert landscape.

As they traveled farther south, the road turned west. No headlights shone behind them and no one pulled out in front of them to block their escape. Soon, they passed the rubble of a small deserted village.

T-Mac drove past quickly.

Kinsley turned in her seat, looking out behind them. "Why didn't we stop there?"

"That was the first place we could hide. If the terrorists figure out we took one of their vehicles and headed south by the only road in this area, that would be the first place they'd look."

She nodded. "True."

"We should be getting into more hills the farther west we go."

"Can't we pass into Ethiopia? Would it be safer for us to travel back to Camp Lemonnier that way?"

"Al-Shabaab doesn't care about borders, but that's the plan for now. After what I did to them, they'll be hoppin' mad and out for blood."

"Other than the three explosions, which were bad enough, should I ask what you did that was so bad?"

He shook his head. "No. But they are three men fewer."

Kinsley shrugged out of her heavy body-armor

vest and laid it on the floorboard. "Here, let me get your helmet."

He lifted his chin, keeping his eyes on the road.

Kinsley unbuckled the chin strap and slid the helmet off his head, without blocking his view of the road in front of him.

She would have offered to help him with his vest, but that would require more effort and he'd need to stop to pull it off. He'd have to wear the heavy plates until they came to a full stop long enough to remove it.

The road grew steeper as they climbed into the hills in northwest Somalia. Soon, they found a turn-off to the north, taking them deeper into rugged terrain, the road turning into more of a path than one used for four-wheeled vehicles.

T-Mac pulled the truck in behind a giant boulder that had fallen from an overhanging cliff. He checked the gas gauge before turning off the engine. "We have three quarters of a tank left. Whatever we do tomorrow, we might have to find more fuel, or find a way to contact my unit for a pickup. But for tonight, we camp here."

Sitting so close to T-Mac for the past two hours, Kinsley had felt a shiver of awareness and anticipation ripple across her skin. Alone in a vehicle with T-Mac was one thing. Alone lying under the stars with the navy SEAL was entirely different.

She gulped back her sudden nerves and blurted,

"Let's see what we have in the back." Kinsley started to reach over Agar to open the passenger door.

T-Mac opened his door first. "Come out this way."

Since getting out the other side would be more difficult with Agar in the way, Kinsley followed T-Mac out the driver's side. Before she could step down from the truck, T-Mac grabbed her around the waist and lifted her out to stand on two feet. Agar jumped down behind her and wandered off to sniff at the rocks and brambles.

T-Mac didn't release her immediately, his hands resting on her hips. "You don't know how crazy it made me when I didn't see your red light."

She laughed. "Trust me. Had you been the one waiting the entire time things were blowing up in that camp, you would have gone off the deep end." Kinsley cupped his cheek and stared at him in the starlight. "You don't know how glad I was when I saw those three blinks of your flashlight."

"What took you so long to respond?" He brushed a strand of her hair out of her face.

"Agar and I got excited when he heard the rumble of the truck's engine. He jerked his lead, and I dropped the handle. I had to grab it before he took off after the oncoming truck. At that point, I didn't know if you were the driver, or someone else." She smiled up at him.

"Well, I was pretty happy to see your red lens shining back at me." He touched her cheek with his fingers and kissed her forehead. "I almost turned around and headed back into that mess."

She pressed her hand over his on her face. "Are you crazy? They would have killed you."

"I thought I'd missed you, or gone out of the camp in the wrong direction."

She laughed, the sound shaky in the night. "Need help getting out of your body armor?"

"I can do it myself," he said.

She laughed. "And where would the fun be in that?" She reached for the fasteners, unbuckling them one at a time. When she had them free, she shoved the vest over his shoulders.

He caught it and laid it on the floorboard of the vehicle and then turned to face her, captured her hands in his and lifted them to his lips. "You amaze me."

She shook her head. "I don't know why. You're the one doing all the heavy lifting on this gig."

"You hold your own, no matter the situation. Most females I know would fall apart."

"Then you don't know the right females." She lifted her chin. "I joined the army, not a sorority."

He laughed and took one of her hands in his. "Come on—let's see what they were loading in the back of the truck."

Kinsley liked the sound of his laughter and the way his hand felt wrapped around hers. No, she wasn't a scared little girl needing the protection of a big burly man, but she liked having T-Mac around. And he had a way of making her feel more feminine than she'd felt in a long time. Kinsley knew she was a strong and courageous soldier. Somewhere along the line, she'd had to bury the woman inside in order to fit in in a man's world. T-Mac brought out the desire and longing she thought she'd never feel again.

And he was a navy SEAL and she was an army soldier. In no scenario could they be together for the long haul. Being with him on a dangerous mission in middle-of-nowhere Africa brought it home to her that they might not be in it for the long run. They might not make it to morning. Every minute they were together now was a gift that should not be squandered.

So she reveled in the touch of his hand. They couldn't hold hands on Camp Lemonnier. Someone would see and report them for fraternization. But out in the hills of Somalia, where every day could be their last, no one was watching. No one would know.

Feeling only a little guilty, Kinsley was also titillated and anxious to see what would happen next. Especially since they would be alone all night.

Chapter Eleven

At the back of the vehicle, T-Mac hit the switch on his flashlight and shone it up into the back of the large utility truck. He reluctantly released Kinsley's hand and passed the flashlight to her to hold while he lowered the tailgate.

The back of the truck contained crates and boxes.

T-Mac climbed up into the truck bed and picked through, opening boxes, moving some and setting others to the side.

"These cardboard boxes are full of food and rations marked WHO."

"World Health Organization," Kinsley said. "They must be stealing food and medical supplies destined for refugee camps."

"The wooden crates aren't marked WHO and they weren't destined for refugee camps." His gut knotted as he lifted out a brand new M4A1 rifle and held it up for her to see. "We definitely found the opposite end of the snake, selling illegal arms to the enemy."

Kinsley shone the flashlight away from the boxes

for a moment and then back into the bed of the truck. "Holy crap, T-Mac. You need to see this." She pointed to the rear bumper of the truck.

T-Mac dropped down out of the vehicle and stood beside Kinsley as she pointed the flashlight at a smear of black spray paint half covering numbers and letters stenciled onto the desert-tan paint.

"You've got to be kidding." T-Mac rubbed at the paint covering the numbers. "That's one of ours from the motor pool."

Kinsley nodded. "And those M4 rifles?"

"The armory isn't missing any, that we've heard of, but they're the same style and military grade as what is issued to our soldiers. Plus, they have the bullets to go with them. I saw someone drop a case in the middle of the camp."

"Great. Someone is arming Al-Shabaab with our own weapons." Kinsley rubbed her arms, as if trying to chase away the chilly night air. "I get that people would be able to sell weapons directly to our enemies, but how would Al-Shabaab get their hands on one of our vehicles without us hearing about it?"

"All the more reason for us to get back to Camp Lemonnier…with the evidence."

"Right." Kinsley tilted her head toward the back of the truck. "I don't suppose you found any blankets or immediately edible food in that truck, did you?"

T-Mac shook his head. "Sorry. Only guns, rice and medical supplies on this truck."

Kinsley dug into the pockets on her uniform pants

and in her jacket. "Fortunately, I brought some protein bars and some snacks for Agar."

He took one of the protein bars and held it up to the flashlight. "Are you always this prepared?"

"I've learned to be." She reached into another pocket for a ziplock bag of food for Agar. "I know myself and Agar. We work better when we're not hungry."

"Good to know," T-Mac said. "We should get a little sleep before dawn. We might be out here for a day if the terrorists take their time moving from their previous location."

Kinsley glanced around at the rock outcroppings nearby. "I can stay awake and stand guard for the first shift."

"There's not much of the night left."

"You've been driving and did all of the work setting off those charges. I'm sure you're exhausted. You need to recharge."

"I'm fine," T-Mac assured her. "I've gotten by on a lot less sleep. You sleep first."

She frowned. "Only if you wake me in a couple hours so that I can pull guard duty while you get a little rest." She crossed her arms over her chest and raised her brows, waiting.

He sighed. "Okay. But for now you need to find a place to sleep."

"How about in the cab of the truck?" she suggested. "The bench seat is the softest thing around, and if we need to make a quick escape, we don't have to make a dash for it."

"Good thinking." He held the passenger door for her.

"I'll sleep behind the wheel," Kinsley insisted. "That way you can stretch out beside me without any obstructions."

"You mean, if we have to beat a hasty retreat, you'll do the driving?" He grinned and let her get in first.

"If I have to, I will." Kinsley slid across the seat to the driver's side. When he didn't get in, she stared out at him. "What's wrong?"

"Nothing. I just figured Agar needed a warm place to sleep. He needs some rest, too." He patted the dog's head and then leaned the seat forward, opening up the back seat for a passenger. "He worked hard tonight."

Kinsley smiled at how easily Agar got along with T-Mac. She gave the dog the command to climb up into the vehicle.

Agar leaped up and settled on the floorboard between the driver's and passenger's side.

Kinsley reached back to pat the animal's head.

When T-Mac still hesitated with his hand on the door, Kinsley frowned. "Aren't you getting in?"

"I think I'd be better off standing guard in the open where I can see someone coming."

Kinsley's frown deepened. "Would it make any difference if I said I need you with me?"

His lips turned upward on the corners. "It might."

She shook her head. "Then please, stay."

"For the record, I don't think it's a good idea."

She smiled. "For the record, I agree. But we're out here alone. The only people who will know or care will be us." Kinsley patted the seat beside her. "You need rest, even if you don't sleep."

"I've been sitting for the past couple of hours while driving."

She raised her brow. "Fine. Suit yourself. I'm going to get some sleep so I can take the next shift." She leaned back against the seat and closed her eyes.

T-Mac stood in the open door of the truck, staring at Kinsley, knowing that if he got into the truck, he might not be able to keep his hands to himself.

The woman was sexy without trying. She tipped back her head, exposing the long line of her very pretty, and kissable, neck.

His lips tingled, and he longed to press them to the pulse beating at the base of her throat.

Her lips tipped upward at the corners and she chuckled. "You might as well get in and close the door. It gets cold at night in the desert." The husky tone of her voice made his groin tighten.

Getting into the truck beside Kinsley was a very bad idea when all T-Mac wanted to do was touch her, taste her and kiss her until they both begged for air.

Despite what his head was telling him, T-Mac followed his gut. Or was it his heart? Whatever. He climbed into the truck and sat beside Kinsley.

She tilted her head toward him and opened one eye. "That wasn't so hard, was it?"

"Sweetheart, you have no idea," he murmured.

She closed her eyes and sighed. "Wake me in two hours."

T-Mac forced himself to stare straight ahead. But every time Kinsley shifted, he couldn't help glancing her way.

Her head fell back against the headrest, tipped at an uncomfortable-looking angle.

Before he could think better of it, he found himself saying, "It might be more comfortable lying across the seat."

She gave a weak smile. "Thanks. I've never been very good at sleeping sitting up." Kinsley tipped over and tried to fit herself between the driver's door and T-Mac's thigh.

"Seriously." He snorted. "You can lay your head on my thigh. I promise not to bite."

Kinsley sat up, frowning. "Are you sure? I don't want to make you uncomfortable."

"Oh, babe, I'm way past uncomfortable." He shook his head. "Just use my leg as a pillow."

"But I don't want to make you uncom—" she started again.

"Woman, are you always so argumentative?" He gripped her shoulders and pulled her across his lap. "You can't help but make me crazy, and you don't even have to touch me to accomplish that." He kissed her lips hard and then lifted his head. "I've wanted to do that since we stopped. And I want to do so much more. But this is neither the time nor the place." He sighed and leaned his forehead against hers. "You're an amazing woman, and I want so much more than just a kiss."

Kinsley's eyes widened. "Oh." Then she snuggled into him. "What's stopping you? Because it sure as hell isn't me." She cupped his face between her palms and kissed him. She pulled back until her mouth was only a breath away from his, and then whispered, "It could be a very long night, or far too short. Depends on how you spend it."

T-Mac didn't need more of an invitation than that. "You realize we'll be breaking all the rules?"

"Damn the rules." She kissed him again, this time pushing her tongue past his teeth to slide along the length of his.

T-Mac held her close, his heart pounding against his ribs. After all that had happened and that short amount of time he'd thought he'd lost her...he couldn't hold back. He had to hold her, touch her, bury himself in her.

Her fingers flew across the buttons on his jacket, popping them free of the buttonholes one at a time. When she had his jacket open, she ran her fingers across his chest, the warmth of her hands burning through the fabric of his T-shirt.

He slipped his hand beneath her uniform jacket and smoothed it up her back and down to the base of her spine. "Once we start down this path, I can't guarantee I can stop."

"I don't want you to stop. I want you, Trace McGuire. We might not have tomorrow, but we can make good use of tonight."

"What about not getting involved with a navy guy?"

"Tonight, we're neither army nor navy. We're just two people, alone in the hills."

He chuckled and brushed a kiss across the tip of her nose. "And what happens in the hills stays in the hills?"

Kinsley nodded. "Something like that." She raised her hands to her own uniform jacket and pushed the top button free. "Now, are you going to talk, or are we going to make out?"

He laughed out loud and pulled her into his arms. "I feel like a teen on his first date. All we need is a cheesy song to play and a cop to shine his light into the window."

She smiled. "I can do without the cop with the flashlight, but we can make our own music."

"I like the way you think, Army."

"I like the way you feel, Navy."

He helped her with the rest of her buttons and pushed the jacket over her shoulders.

They became a tangle of hands and clothing in an effort to remove the T-shirts.

All the wiggling on his lap made him even harder and more desperate to be with her.

When she reached behind her back to unclip her bra, he pushed her hands aside and flicked the hooks loose and then slid the bra from her shoulders and down her arms.

Her small, perky breasts spilled into his hands.

Kinsley inhaled deeply, pressing more firmly into T-Mac's palms. She cupped the backs of his hands and held him there. "You don't know how good that feels."

He chuckled. "Oh, I think I do."

Kinsley shifted her legs until she straddled his hips and slid her center over his growing erection.

"Darlin', it doesn't work that way."

"What?" she asked, her voice breathy, as if she couldn't get enough air past her vocal cords.

"We have too much between us."

Kinsley sighed. "I know. Can we hurry the fore-play along? I'm not a very patient person."

T-Mac set her away from him. In a flurry of awk-ward movements, bumping into the windows, doors and each other, they got naked and spread their cloth-ing out on the seat.

By then, T-Mac was breathing hard, his body on fire from touching hers so many times in the process of undressing.

"Uh, this could be a bad time to ask," Kinsley started, "but I don't suppose you brought protec-tion?" She laughed nervously. "I mean, it's not like you think about things like that when you're gearing up. I wouldn't expect you to have anything like that. I know I didn't think to pack it."

T-Mac sealed her mouth with a kiss. "Knowing you were on this mission, I packed extra first-aid supplies and even tossed in some protection. Don't ask me why. My gut instinct has never steered me wrong."

"Hear, hear for your gut." She kissed him hard and once again straddled his hips, skimming her already wet entrance over his rock-hard staff. "So, where is it?"

"You were serious about skipping the foreplay," he said.

"Damn right. Life's short—you have go for what you want… Be in the moment. You never know when fate will hand you a treasure or stab you in the heart."

"Speaking from experience?" he asked softly.

She nodded. The starlight shining in through the window glinted off moisture in her eyes.

He gripped her arms. "Did you lose someone you cared about?"

Again, she nodded without speaking.

His heart wrenched and he asked the question he wasn't certain he wanted the answer to. "Someone you loved?"

KINSLEY HAD SPENT the past two years trying to heal her broken heart and pushing past her fear of losing someone she cared about enough to let herself fall in love again. She thought she was well on her way to doing just that, until she'd hunkered down outside an Al-Shabaab camp, waiting for T-Mac to appear. All that old fear and anxiety had surfaced and practically consumed her.

Now that T-Mac was safe and in her arms, she couldn't let another moment go by without really being with him. She'd spoken her truth about seizing the moment. They might not have tomorrow together. If Al-Shabaab caught up with them, or the rules of Camp Lemonnier kept them apart, they would have only this one moment in time to pack into their memories. Kinsley was determined to make the most of it.

Their military careers would keep them apart tomorrow, but they had the night.

Kinsley held out her hand. "If you'll hand me the protection, we can get this show on the road."

T-Mac shook his head. "Not so fast. You might not think foreplay is necessary, but I want you to be every bit as turned on as I am before I come into you."

A shiver of anticipation rippled across her skin. "What exactly did you have in mind?"

"This." In one fluid motion, he turned her over and pinned her to the seat and cushion of clothing.

She giggled. "Are you always so eager with your women?"

T-Mac kissed her forehead and the tip of her nose, and nibbled her left earlobe before replying. "Just so you know, I don't have women. I'm not celibate, but there's no woman in my life except the one lying beneath me at this moment."

Her body heated at his warm, resonant tone. "I'd understand if you had a female in every port."

"That's nice. But I don't." He trailed kisses down the side of her throat and lingered at the base, where her pulse beat hard and fast.

Kinsley squirmed beneath him, wanting more than just his lips, more than kisses.

Then he moved down her body, trailing his mouth, his tongue and his hands. He slowed to suck one of her nipples between his teeth and rolled it around.

She arched her back off the seat, pressing her body closer, a moan rising up her throat.

He flicked the hardened bud of her nipple with his tongue again and again. Then he moved to take the other nipple into his mouth and gave it the same delicious treatment.

Kinsley's core tightened, coiled and heated. She threaded her hands in his hair, urging him to take more.

He did, pulling hard on her breast, alternating between flicking and nipping at the tip.

Then he abandoned her breasts and moved lower, skimming across her ribs, tonguing a warm trail, stopping to dip into her belly button. When he reached her mound of curls, he parted her folds and dragged his finger across that strip of flesh tightly packed with nerves.

A moan rose up Kinsley's throat, and she dug her fingernails into his scalp. "Oh…dear…sweet…"

He touched her there with the tip of his tongue.

Kinsley moaned again, her hips rising to meet that tongue, willing him to do that again.

T-Mac swept a warm, wet path through her folds and dipped a finger into her slick channel.

Her entire body quivering, Kinsley ached for what came next. She wanted him. Inside her. Now.

But he wasn't finished with her. Apparently, he wanted to torture her into submission, one incredibly delicious lick or stroke at a time.

His tongue worked magic on her nubbin while his fingers teased her entrance and dipped in, first one, then another until three stretched her opening, preparing her for him.

Tension built inside, centering at her core. Her muscles tightened and she dug her feet into the seat cushion, pressing upward. "Please," she begged.

"Please what?"

"I want you."

He chuckled, his warm breath playing across her wetness. "Sweetheart, you have me."

"No. Now. Inside me," she said, her voice breathy. She couldn't breathe, she was so caught up in the sensations he evoked. "I need you."

"But you're not there yet." He blew a stream of warm air across her nubbin and then flicked it with his tongue.

A shock of electricity ripped through her from the point where T-Mac touched her all the way out to the tips of her fingers, tingling all the way.

He flicked again and again, refusing to let up and

give her a chance to fill her lungs, think or pull herself together. She came apart at the seams, rocketing to the stratosphere, any modesty left in the dust of the African desert gone. She soared into the heavens, crying out his name as she launched.

For a long moment, she remained suspended, somewhere between earth and heaven, every nerve on fire, her blood moving like molten lava through her veins.

When she finally came back to earth, she tugged on T-Mac's hair. "Now. I need you now," she said, her voice hoarse with emotion.

He crawled up her body, leaned up on his knees and grabbed the foil package he'd set on the dash earlier. He tore open one end and shook out the protection into his palm.

Impatient, and past caring how pushy she looked, Kinsley snatched the item from his palm and rolled it over his distended erection.

When he was fully sheathed, she positioned him between her legs.

T-Mac took over, pressing against her entrance, his gaze meeting hers. "Tell me to stop, and I will." He gave her a crooked grin. "It'll be hard, but I can walk away if you change your mind."

Before he finished talking, she was already shaking her head. "You're not walking away now." She gripped his buttocks in both hands and pulled him closer. He penetrated her, easing in, careful not to hurt her, giving her channel time to adjust to his girth.

The deliberateness was excruciating. More painful than anything, and she could do nothing to stop it. She almost pounded her forehead in frustration. Why did he insist on going so slowly? Gripping his bottom, she guided him in and out, setting a rhythm both comforting and exciting.

T-Mac drove deep, filling her to completely full, stretching her inside and creating a friction so wonderful, it set her body on fire.

She urged him to go faster and faster, until he pounded into her like a piston.

Kinsley rose up to greet each thrust with one of her own. The slapping sound of skin on skin echoed inside the truck cab.

T-Mac's body stiffened. He thrust one last time, going as deep as he could get and froze, his shaft pulsing with his release. His breathing came in ragged breaths, his chest heaving, a sheen of perspiration making his body glisten in the starlight penetrating through the windshield.

When at last he relaxed, he lay down on her, covering her body with his. He gathered her in his arms and kissed her long, hard and thoroughly, stealing her breath away and caressing her tongue.

When at last he eased off to let her fill her lungs again, she let go of a shaky laugh. "Wow."

He chuckled. "That's all? Just *wow*?"

"You so rocked my world, my brain is mush and my vocabulary reduced to one-syllable words. Thus…*wow*."

He lifted her off the seat, removed the condom and settled his body on the cushion, draping her over his chest. "This way I don't crush you."

"I'd die a happy death." She laid her head against his heart and listened to the fast, steady rhythm. "Think Al-Shabaab will find us tonight?"

"I doubt it," he said.

"Good." Her fingers curled softly into his chest. "Then you can stay with me."

He rested his hand over hers. "Someone needs to stay awake in case they find us."

"I'm willing to risk it if you are."

He inhaled deeply, the movement raising her up and then lowering her downward. "Much as I'd like to lay here with you and feel your body against mine all night, I'd better get out there and keep both eyes open."

She sighed. "Wake me in an hour and a half. I'll take the next watch."

He didn't answer, just shifted into a sitting position, levering her across his lap. He cupped her breasts in his palms. "You know, you're beautiful beneath all that camouflage."

She wiggled against his stiff erection. "You're not so bad yourself." Kinsley leaned into his palms. "Care to go for round two?"

"I'd love to, but I only had the one condom."

"It's too bad we're not close to a drugstore." She cupped his cheeks and bussed his lips with a hard kiss. "Thank you."

He smiled. "For what?"

"For not being selfish, and making it just as good for me as it was for you." Kinsley frowned. "It was good for you, wasn't it?"

"Darlin', if it had been any better, I would be passed out or dead from a heart attack." He lifted her off his lap and set her on the seat beside him. He dragged on his trousers and boots and then slipped out the passenger door to stand on the ground.

Kinsley dressed in her bra, T-shirt and panties, her gaze on T-Mac as he covered his glorious body one item of clothing at a time. What a shame that he had to cover all that taut skin and those bulging muscles.

She dragged her trousers up her legs and buttoned them, then pulled on her boots with a sigh. They were back in uniform, back to reality. Soon, they would be back at Camp Lemonnier, where they wouldn't even be able to hold hands or kiss without the threat of an Article 15.

"Sleep. You don't know what tomorrow might bring," T-Mac said. "You'll need your strength." He left her alone in the truck and disappeared around the giant boulder to take up a position where he could watch the road.

With a yawn, Kinsley leaned over the back of the seat to check on Agar.

He lifted his nose and touched her hand.

"At least I will have you after the SEALs redeploy back to the States."

Agar nudged her hand and licked her fingers.

There had been a time when she thought loving Agar was enough. His loyalty was unquestioned, his love unconditional. But he wasn't a man. Kinsley hadn't realized just how much she needed the warmth and physical contact only a man could give her.

Until T-Mac entered her life.

She hadn't known what she was missing.

Now she did. And he would ship out, leaving a giant hole in her heart and soul.

She lay on the seat, her head resting on her bent arm. A single tear slipped from the corner of her eye and splashed onto the seat.

Crying accomplished nothing. So she limited it to the one tear. When T-Mac was gone, she might have to shed a few more. Until then, she wouldn't think that far ahead.

Chapter Twelve

T-Mac didn't wake Kinsley after an hour and a half. Nor did he wake her at two hours. Not a single vehicle had gone by on the road. He couldn't be certain one hadn't passed while he was making love to Kinsley, but he doubted it.

Which meant the Al-Shabaab faction hadn't made it out of the camp at a decent hour, unless they'd slipped by him while he'd been otherwise occupied.

He cursed himself for losing his concentration and focus. Their lives depended on him staying aware and on top of the situation. Sex in a truck wasn't going to keep them alive.

But oh, it had felt amazing. Having Kinsley in his arms hadn't gotten her out of his system. If anything, holding her made him want her even more.

The woman was tough as nails on the outside and all soft and vulnerable on the inside. And she'd fit perfectly against him, their bodies seemingly made for each other.

He found himself trying to figure out how a navy

SEAL and an army dog handler could make a long-distance relationship work. Throughout the night, he worked it over in his mind and came to one conclusion. As long as they were both on active duty, a relationship between them was doomed before it started.

Who was he kidding? They would never be on the same base, and probably not in the same state or even the same continent. Why go through the heartache of separation, as often as he was on call and deployed?

Why was he even thinking that way? He was a navy SEAL. He didn't have any right to expect a woman to give up all she knew and loved to follow him around the country or world, only to be stuck somewhere, waiting for him to come home.

He'd been an idiot to make love to her. Satisfying his base needs could only hurt her in the long run. And make it harder to let go when he left.

A couple times during the night, he'd almost nodded off. Each time, he'd imagine Kinsley wearing a dress, standing in the doorway of a cute little cottage with a white picket fence, sending him off or welcoming him home.

But that image clashed with the reality of what and who she was. She'd trained to be a dog handler. Surely, she would never be content to stay behind and keep the home fires burning.

He admired his teammates' ability to find love and the ways they'd worked out the difficulties of maintaining a relationship even when they were separated. If they could do it, why not him?

Because Kinsley belonged to the army. She had a commitment to serve. She couldn't move around from navy base to navy base and still do what she did. The army didn't care if she was married to a navy guy. They'd send her wherever they needed her.

T-Mac wished Big Jake or Harm were there. He could sure use some advice, or just a sounding board. He had a lot on his mind and he couldn't seem to push any of it aside.

The first gray light of dawn pushed over the tops of the hills, creating long shadows and warming the air.

They needed to get on the road to Djibouti. The sooner the better. He'd made up his mind that they would take the route through Ethiopia, hopefully avoiding Al-Shabaab all together.

As much as he hated doing it, he got up, brushed off the dust and walked back to the truck to wake Kinsley.

When he looked inside, the truck was empty. His heart leaped into his throat and he shot a glance around the truck, the cliff and the giant boulder. Kinsley was nowhere to be seen.

With his heart pounding and a sweat breaking out on his forehead, T-Mac spun in a circle.

"I'm over here," Kinsley called out, emerging from around another, smaller boulder. "I had to relieve myself."

T-Mac didn't answer, taking a moment to drag air

back into his lungs and calm his racing pulse. "You scared me."

She smiled. "I'm sorry. I didn't think about letting you know."

"It's imperative that you let me know where you are at all times. Al-Shabaab isn't above kidnapping women, drugging them and abusing them. They will give you even less slack because you are dressed as a soldier."

Kinsley squared her shoulders. "Bring it on."

T-Mac frowned. "You can't take on all of the Al-Shabaab faction. They have weapons, and they aren't afraid to use them. They don't follow any government. They aren't governed by the Geneva convention and they don't have a code of honor like ours."

Kinsley crossed her arms over her chest. "I can take care of myself, navy guy."

He cupped her chin. "You might think you can. But if these men gang up on you, you have to be ready for the worst."

She pushed her shoulders back and lifted her chin. "Yes, sir." Then she leaned her face into his open palm. "I'll play it safe."

"Good." He bent to kiss her, unable to resist her lips, swollen from his kisses. "What am I going to do with you?"

"I asked myself the same question all night long," she admitted.

He stared down into her eyes.

Kinsley met his gaze, unblinking. "How do two

people from two totally separate military branches even dare to get together? You have to be all kinds of stupid to allow it to happen."

He chuckled. "Call me stupid."

"And me." She turned her face and pressed a kiss into his palm. "But we can't get hung up on what's going on here."

"You're right," he agreed. "We have to get back to Camp Lemonnier and report what we found in that Al-Shabaab camp."

"Right." She cupped the back of his hand. "And what happened here, last night, will stay here." Her lips twisted into a tight frown. "It can't go any further."

T-Mac wanted to disagree. He opened his mouth to do just that, but closed it nearly as fast. Kinsley was right. They couldn't go there. Anything between them was doomed. "You're right. We have a job to do. We need to focus on getting it done."

Though he knew it would only prolong the pain, he pulled her into his arms and kissed her hard.

At first she stood stiffly. Then her hands slid up the back of his neck and cupped his head, pulling him closer. She opened to him, allowing him to sweep in and caress her tongue with his. He accepted her offering, greedily tasting her, holding her and giving back all she gave him.

Agar brought them back to their senses. He pressed a warm, wet nose between them.

Kinsley leaned back and laughed shakily. "Hey,

boy. Are you not getting the attention you deserve?" She lowered her hand to his head and scratched him behind the ears.

T-Mac dropped his hands lower, cupping the small of her back. He leaned forward and kissed her forehead, then swept his mouth lightly across her lips. Then he stepped away. "We have to get going. The sooner we get back, or find a phone to call for a lift, the better."

Kinsley pressed a hand to her lips and nodded. "I'm ready."

Agar jumped up into the cab of the truck and sat in the middle between Kinsley and T-Mac.

T-Mac would have preferred Kinsley sitting beside him, but having the dog between them was perhaps the only way he'd keep his hands off the woman.

He needed to concentrate on the road ahead, not on the woman. The men from the Al-Shabaab site would be out for revenge and wouldn't stop short of killing the people responsible for setting off the explosions in their camp and offing three of their men.

T-Mac turned the key in the ignition. The engine didn't make a sound. He did it again with the same result. Damn.

Kinsley held up a hand. "Pop the hood."

"I'll look," he insisted.

"No, you need to turn the key. I had some training in the motor pool. Let me try the usual quick fixes." She hopped out of the truck and ran around to the front.

T-Mac released the hood. Kinsley pushed it up and climbed on the bumper to lean over the engine.

T-Mac tried to see what she was doing, but the hood blocked his vision.

"Try it now," she called out.

He turned the key, and the engine started right away.

Kinsley closed the hood and climbed up into the passenger seat with a grin.

"What was wrong?" he asked as he shifted into Drive and pulled around the big boulder.

"Corrosion on the battery terminals. All I did was wiggle them and break loose some of the crud. If we stop again soon, we need to do a more thorough job of cleaning the posts and connectors."

T-Mac admired the female for her ingenuity. He knew too many who wouldn't have had a clue about engines. "You are an amazing woman, Kinsley."

She shook her head. "Not at all. I just use the brain I have."

T-Mac's chest tightened. The more he knew about her, the more he loved. When the time came to part, he'd have a tough time saying goodbye.

KINSLEY SAT IN the passenger seat with her hand on Agar's back. The dog usually had a way of calming her when she was upset. All she had to do was rest her hand on his fur and the world would right itself.

Not this time. Since losing Jason to an IED explosion, she hadn't thought she'd fall for another military guy. Too much could go wrong and her heart couldn't take another loss like that.

She'd dated Jason for two years and thought she was in love with him, but what she felt for T-Mac seemed much stronger and harder to push aside.

Who would have thought she'd find a man who could rival Jason? Or that she would fall so fast and so hard? She was insane to even consider another relationship with a guy so entrenched in his military career.

No. Just no.

She stared at the road ahead as they angled west toward the border between Somalia and Ethiopia without actually seeing any of the terrain. Her thoughts remained pinned to the man in the driver's seat. In her peripheral vision, she could see him over Agar's head.

T-Mac's lips pressed tightly together, and his hands gripped the steering wheel as he kept the truck on the dirt road, his gaze sweeping the road ahead, the hills to each side and the rearview mirror.

He had a strong jaw and high cheekbones to go with his auburn hair and the dark auburn shadow of his beard.

If they somehow managed to get together, they'd have beautiful redheaded children. She could imagine a little girl with bright hair and T-Mac's startling blue eyes. And a little boy with auburn hair and her green eyes.

Kinsley looked straight ahead. Why was she day-dreaming the impossible?

As soon as the SEAL team left, T-Mac would forget she ever existed.

She wouldn't forget him. Not for a long time. But she'd get on with her life, complete her commitment to the army and decide what she wanted to do next. She loved training dogs. Maybe she'd start her own training and boarding facility. And when Agar was retired from duty, she'd apply to adopt him. He deserved a happy forever home. A place with a big yard and lots of room to run and explore.

The truck leaped forward, jerking Kinsley out of her reverie.

"What's wrong?" she asked.

T-Mac's lips thinned and he glanced in the side mirror. "We've got trouble behind us."

Kinsley turned in her seat and stared through the back window, over the boxes and crates. Emerging from the dust cloud behind them were a truck and two motorcycles. The men riding the motorcycles wore the black garb of the Al-Shabaab fighters.

Her pulse banging against her veins, Kinsley fumbled on the floorboard for her rifle.

The truck bounced on the rough dirt road.

T-Mac pushed the accelerator all the way to the floor, but the truck and the motorcycles behind them were catching up.

"Stay down!" he shouted over the roar of the road noise. "They have guns."

No sooner had the word *guns* left his mouth than a bullet hit the back window and exited through the front, leaving a perfect round hole in each.

"Get down!" T-Mac ordered.

"The hell I will." Kinsley crawled over the back seat.

"What are you doing? You're going to get killed."

"No, but I'm going to put the hurt on them." She hit the bullet hole in the window with the butt of her weapon. The glass shattered, but didn't fall. She hit it again. This time shards spilled outside and onto the seat beside her.

Bashing the jagged shards again and again, she cleared the rear window, pointed the rifle through the open space and aimed at the vehicles following them.

One of the motorcycles raced up to the back of the truck.

Though she was being jostled by the bumps in the road, Kinsley steadied her arm as much as possible and stared down the sights at the man on the motorcycle, who was getting close enough that he could eventually hop into the truck.

She took a breath, held it and caressed the trigger.

Her aim was true. The man on the motorcycle jerked sideways, lying over the bike, skidding along the dirt road for a long way before coming to a stop.

"One down!" T-Mac called. "Good shot."

Kinsley didn't respond, her attention on the other motorcycle and truck.

The motorcycle had slowed to run alongside the truck, both of which were speeding toward them.

Kinsley aimed for the driver's window.

Just as she pulled the trigger, their truck hit a rut, throwing her aim off. The bullet went wide.

Undisturbed, she aimed again and pulled the trigger before they hit another bump.

The bullet must have hit close to the driver. He swerved, sending the truck off the side of the road for a moment before straightening and pulling back into the middle.

The motorcycle stayed on the road, gained ground and headed for the driver's side of T-Mac's truck.

Kinsley took aim, sighted down the barrel and pulled the trigger.

The weapon jammed.

"Damn!"

"What?" T-Mac asked.

"Jam." She slapped the magazine from the bottom and pulled the trigger again. Still jammed.

The motorcycle rider pulled alongside the truck. "Watch out!" she called. "Motorcycle coming up on your side." Kinsley pulled back the bolt and found a bullet lodged at a bad angle. She dug in her pocket for the knife she kept handy. She dug out the bullet, slammed the bolt home and rolled down the window in the back seat as the motorcycle rider pulled up beside the truck, holding a handgun.

Kinsley aimed through the window and pulled the trigger.

The weapon jammed again.

Her heart hammering, Kinsley turned the weapon around, leaned out the window and, holding the barrel, used the rifle like a baseball bat and swung as hard as she could, knocking the handgun from the rider's hands and the rider from his seat. He crashed to the ground, the motorcycle slipping sideways under the truck's wheels.

The resulting bump nearly threw Kinsley out of the truck. She was so concerned about keeping hold of her rifle, she forgot to hold on to something to keep from being thrown from the truck. Thankfully, she had her heel hooked beneath the back seat and was able to pull herself and her rifle back inside.

Just in time for the truck behind them to ram into the rear of their vehicle.

Kinsley slammed into the back of T-Mac's seat.

"Are you okay?" he asked.

She pulled herself off the floorboard and up onto the seat, shaken but not injured. "I'm okay."

Then she cleared her weapon, braced it on the rim of the back window, aimed at the driver's windshield and prayed her rifle wouldn't jam.

The trailing vehicle raced forward, full speed.

Kinsley focused down the sights and pulled the trigger.

The bullet flew through the window and into the truck, directly into the driver's-side windshield.

For a moment, the vehicle stayed its course, heading straight for the back of T-Mac's truck.

Kinsley braced for impact, closed her eyes and held on.

A moment passed. Then two. Nothing happened. The truck behind them didn't hit theirs.

Frowning, Kinsley opened her eyes.

The Al-Shabaab vehicle was going so fast that when it spun sideways, it rolled over and over, coming to a halt on its side. Steam rose from the engine, but no one crawled out.

Drawing in a deep breath, Kinsley stared out the back window until the toppled truck became a speck in the distance. She crawled over the seat and settled in the front, her weapon across her lap.

Agar nudged her hand.

She laughed and patted his head, glad she was still alive to do it.

"You weren't kidding when you said you were a good shot," T-Mac said.

"I'm just lucky you were able to keep your cool and drive on."

"We make a good team," T-Mac said.

"Yes," Kinsley agreed. Too bad the military wouldn't keep them together to see how far they'd go on synergy.

Hell, too bad they wouldn't be together for the long haul. But Kinsley couldn't be too sad. Not after what had just happened. At least they were still alive.

Without a tail following them, they drove into Ethiopia, hoping to find a town of sufficient size and infrastructure where they might find a working telephone.

After two hours on the dirt road, they finally entered such a town. And none too soon. The gas gauge had dipped low. Fortunately, there was a place to purchase fuel, and that station had a telephone.

After going through several operators, he got one who understood how to connect him to an operator at Camp Lemonnier, and he was able to talk with his commander.

Kinsley waited nearby, feeling more hopeful than she had since they got separated from the rest of the SEAL team.

When T-Mac completed the call, he smiled in her direction, making her day brighter. "They're sending a helicopter to collect us. They should be here in two hours."

"What about the motor-pool truck?" she asked.

"I mentioned it to Commander Ward. He didn't give a damn about the truck." T-Mac grinned. "He was just glad to hear from us. They sent a couple of Black Hawks out to the site this morning. Everyone was gone."

"We expected that. They were packing up when you hit them with the explosions."

T-Mac nodded. "The commander figured we might have had something to do with the abandoned vehicles and scorched fuel barrels."

"You did a number on them." Kinsley glanced

around the little town. "I don't suppose we could find some food here?" she suggested.

"I'm hungry too, but I'd just as soon wait until we get back to Camp Lemonnier. At least I'll know what I'm eating."

"Agreed." Her belly rumbled loudly. "Where will they land the choppers?"

"On the road headed northeast out of town," T-Mac said. He paid the man for the fuel, thanked him for the use of the phone and held the passenger door while Kinsley climbed up into the cab.

In silence, T-Mac closed the door and climbed into the driver's seat. He sat for a moment with his hand on the key. He opened his mouth as if to say something, but closed it without uttering a word.

Kinsley wondered what he'd been about to say, but didn't ask. Her emotions were still on overload from making love to the man the previous night, followed by the adrenaline rush of being attacked.

If he said anything about forgetting what happened, or pretending it never did, she wasn't sure how she'd react. The only thing she was certain of was that her heart was 100 percent involved.

Dang. She didn't need that kind of complication.

Chapter Thirteen

T-Mac drove a few miles out of the small town and parked the truck in a clear area with only one tree for hundreds of yards. The helicopter would be able to land easily, and T-Mac would be able to watch both directions. If Al-Shabaab decided to send more mercenaries their way, T-Mac needed to see them enough in advance to know whether they should stand fast and defend or run.

For the time being, the road was clear and the sun shone down, burning into the roof of the vehicle, making it unbearably hot inside.

"I'll park in the shade." He positioned the truck beneath the low-hanging branches. Then he climbed down, rounded the hood to the other side and opened the door for Kinsley.

He held out his hand. "We'll be back before you know it."

Kinsley laid her fingers across his palm, but didn't get out of the truck immediately. "About last night…" Her voice was low, husky and sexy as hell.

T-Mac's groin tightened at the mere mention of the previous night. "What about it?"

"We're headed back to camp," she blurted out.

He gave her a tight little smile. "Don't worry, I won't tell anyone. My career is just as much on the line as yours."

She laughed, the sound more nervous than humorous. "No. I mean… I just…" Kinsley flung her hands in the air. "What I'm trying to say is—" She threw herself into his arms and kissed him long and hard.

T-Mac gathered her into his arms and held her in the air, holding her tightly against him, his tongue thrusting between her teeth to sweep across hers.

When he at last lowered her to the ground, he lifted his head and sighed. "We won't get the chance to do that back at the base."

She laughed and leaned her forehead against his chest for a moment. "No, we won't."

He tipped her chin upward. "What are we going to do about us?"

Kinsley shook her head. "I don't think there can be an *us*. Not when we're both on active duty, and we'll be going our separate ways as soon as we leave Djibouti."

"It's hard to believe we've only known each other a few days. I feel like I've known you for a lifetime."

"And I you." She smiled. "And yet, I don't know anything about you. Like what's your favorite color? Do you have any siblings? Are your parents still alive? Where did you grow up?" She cupped his cheek. "None of that matters because I know you here." Her hand moved from his face to his chest. "You're loyal. You care about your team. You take your duty seriously and you love animals. Those are the big things. The rest is just data."

He pressed a kiss to her forehead. "Blue." And kissed the tip of her nose. "You already know I have one sister." He swept his lips across hers. "Yes, my folks are still alive, and before you lost your memory, I told you how I grew up on my father's farm in Nebraska." He held her face between his palms and kissed her lightly. "And I know very little about you, but I know you can fire a rifle, you aren't afraid of going into enemy territory, you can hold your own as a soldier in the army, you care about Agar. You care about your country and you care enough about me to take out a truck driver and two men on motorcycles."

"To be fair, you lit their world on fire with a little C-4." She wrapped her arms around his waist and squeezed gently. "I'll be sad when you leave with your team to redeploy back to the States."

"And I'll be sad when I go." He shook his head. "Maybe we'll see each other back home," he said hopefully.

"The most likely scenario is that you'll be in Virginia, I'll go back to San Antonio or somewhere else equally distant, and we'll get on with our lives and never see each other again."

"Wow, a little negative much?" He brushed a

strand of her hair from her face. "I prefer my version."

"I do, too. But reality is, we're both committed to our careers. We've trained hard to get where we are today. Jetting back and forth across the country or around the world isn't realistic."

"I'll tell you what." He rested his hand on her hips. "If we're both still single—and since I'm a SEAL, I'm pretty sure that'll be the case for me—can we at least meet on the anniversary of our night in Somalia?"

She smiled. "Sure. Why not? But only if we're both single."

"Good. Then I'll have a date." He captured her face in his hands. "But for now I'd like to take advantage of the little bit of time we have alone together to hold you and kiss you."

"I'm in." She snuggled close to him, despite the heat of the desert sun cooking the landscape around them.

Kinsley gave Agar some water from her Camel-Bak thermos. Then the three of them settled on the ground in the shade of the tree and waited for the helicopter to arrive.

Agar slept while T-Mac kissed Kinsley, held her hand and talked.

While they waited for their transport, T-Mac learned Kinsley's favorite color was red, she had no siblings and her father had passed. She liked watching NFL football but sadly wasn't a Dallas Cowboys fan, preferring the Denver Broncos. She grew up in Colorado Springs, Colorado, and joined the army to earn money for college. She stayed because she enjoyed working with the dogs.

"I like camping and fishing but prefer to shoot animals with a camera, not a gun." She leaned her head against his shoulder. "I don't like to dance, because I'm not very good at it, but I do enjoy slow dancing… with the right person."

"And have you met the right person?"

"I won't lie. I fell in love once. I told you about him. He was a dog handler, too. We thought we might one day have a future together." She sighed. "He and his dog had just identified an IED when the ISIS rebel set it off remotely."

"I'm sorry."

She shrugged. "That's part of the reason why I try not to get involved with military guys. What's the use? They might die or be transferred. I don't know if I can go through that heartache again."

"Will you go through that heartache over me?" T-Mac asked, his arm tightening around her shoulder.

"I'm trying really hard not to fall for you." She tipped her head upward to stare into his eyes. "You're making it really hard on me. Can we stick to the facts that don't mean much?"

"Sorry." He raised his hands in surrender. "Continue."

"Where was I?"

"You like slow dancing."

"Right." She took a breath. "There's not much more. I favor daisies over roses, and I enjoy a cold beer on a hot day, like today, and I really like walking in the rain."

"As hot as it is today, I'd enjoy a cold beer and a little rain as well."

"What about you? Ever been in love?" Kinsley asked.

"No," he said. *Until now,* he didn't add. He feared he was falling hopelessly in love with the army dog handler. But telling her would only make it harder for him and for her when they parted. He'd avoided relationships, knowing how hard they were to maintain for a guy in his career field. He'd never been in love. Kinsey tempted him to break all his self-imposed rules. Was what he was feeling for Kinsey love? His heart skipped several beats and then jerked like a jackhammer.

"Do you want a family?"

"Someday, maybe," he replied. "When I'm not shooting bad guys for a living." He could imagine Kinsley's round belly. She'd be beautiful pregnant with their child. The baby girl would have bright strawberry blond hair like her mother and a smile that would melt every male heart.

Kinsley stiffened. "There's a vehicle coming."

T-Mac leaped to his feet and jerked Kinsley up beside him. They both grabbed their rifles and took up defensive positions, using the truck for cover.

A dilapidated truck loaded with bags of grain,

people and livestock trundled by. The folks on the back of the truck waved as they passed.

Kinsley and T-Mac lowered their weapons out of sight and waved back, not letting their guard down completely.

When the truck disappeared and the dust settled, T-Mac and Kinsley sat beneath the tree again.

The afternoon passed entirely too quickly. By the time the helicopter arrived, they were both hungry and ready to be back at Camp Lemonnier, yet T-Mac was sad to leave their little patch of shade where they'd had the time to get to know each other better.

When the chopper came close enough and T-Mac identified it as one belonging to the US, he stepped out of the shade and waved.

The chopper landed and five men jumped out.

"You old son of a gun." Harm was first to greet him, dragging him into a giant bear hug. "We got a little worried about you when we couldn't find you at the Al-Shabaab camp."

"That's right." Diesel gripped his forearm and pulled him into a hug. "Wasn't as much fun going back to camp without our T-Mac."

"How's the guy who stepped on the mine?"

"It was Stucky. They flew him to Ramstein, Germany," Buck said. "He had multiple lacerations and embedded shrapnel, one piece lodged close to one of his eyes. They're trying to get him to a specialist to save the eye."

"Damn. I hope he'll be okay."

"We all hope for the best." Big Jake limped up to T-Mac. "We saw the damage to the camp. Glad you were able to escape. We were confused when your GPS tracker headed deeper into Somalia."

"I didn't want to lose them, so I sacrificed my tracker. Once I planted it on one of their trucks, I stole one of the vehicles they had in their camp and got the heck out."

"This the truck?" Pitbull called out from where he stood by the vehicle.

"It is."

Pitbull shot a glance toward T-Mac. "Who put the bullet holes in it?"

"Three of the Al-Shabaab fighters caught up to us early this morning."

Pitbull shook his head. "I hope they look worse than this truck."

"They're dead." T-Mac grinned. "Our little dog handler is a crack shot."

Kinsley's cheeks flushed.

Diesel held out his hand to Kinsley. "I'm impressed. You can have my back anytime."

She gripped it and shook. "Thanks."

T-Mac busted through Diesel's grip on Kinsley's hand. "Hey, she's my sidekick."

"Yeah, I get that." Diesel shook his hand. "I've got my own sidekick waiting for me back home."

Harm snapped pictures of the truck and the bumper with the writing.

T-Mac walked to the back of the truck and climbed

in. He opened one of the crates and held up an M4A1 rifle. "We can't leave these weapons in the back of that truck. They might fall into the wrong hands."

"Load them into the helicopter," Big Jake said. "We'll take them back to camp for disposal. We need to get back. The commander wants a debrief."

The men loaded the crate of weapons onto the chopper. T-Mac helped Kinsley and Agar up into the fuselage and climbed in to sit beside her. He adjusted her safety harness around her shoulders and lap before buckling his.

"Here." Big Jake handed Kinsley a plastic-wrapped package. "Figured you might be hungry."

"Thank you." Kinsley smiled and opened the package to reveal a sandwich loaded with salami, ham and turkey slices. She moaned.

The sound reminded T-Mac of how she'd moaned when he'd made love to her the night before. His groin tightened and he looked away from her biting into the sandwich.

"We didn't forget you." Big Jake slapped another sandwich into T-Mac's hands. "Eat up. It's a long flight back and the commander won't let you hit the chow hall or the sack until you debrief him on what happened after we left you."

Pitbull faced T-Mac in the seat across from him. He leaned forward and yelled as the rotor blades spun up to speed. "The boss wasn't too happy with us when we came back without the dog handler."

"You didn't have a choice. You had to get Stucky back before he bled out," T-Mac said.

The men settled back against their seats, the roar of the engine and blades making it too difficult to carry on a conversation.

The chopper lifted off the ground and circled back the way it had come.

T-Mac made short work of the sandwich, feeding bits of bread and meat to Agar.

Kinsley ate a third of her sandwich and fed the rest to Agar. Once she finished the food, she stuffed the plastic wrap into her pocket and leaned her head back, closing her eyes. She let her hand fall between them on the seat where T-Mac's rested.

T-Mac captured her hand in his and held on. If someone noticed, too damned bad. That little bit of contact with Kinsley might be the last he would get before they made it back to all the rules and consequences. He'd be damned if he wasted the opportunity to touch her this one last time.

KINSLEY CURLED HER fingers around T-Mac's. Though the past thirty-six hours had been difficult, she hadn't exactly felt scared. Unless she counted the minutes she'd lain in wait for T-Mac to emerge from the rebel camp. Then, she hadn't been afraid for herself, but for T-Mac. He'd walked right into that camp as bold as day and set off those explosions. Anyone could have caught him. Anyone could have shot him on sight.

Kinsley had been more scared than she'd been in

her entire life. She felt as if her heart hadn't started beating again until she'd seen T-Mac behind the wheel of that truck.

Her fingers tightened around his. Now she wanted to hold on to his hand and never let go. She was afraid she'd lose him. Which was silly. Their time together was coming to an end. His team was scheduled to ship out in a day or two. They'd leave and she'd be left behind to continue her mission of supporting operations out of Djibouti. Her deployment was for a full year. She'd been there only a few weeks.

When she'd arrived, she'd been excited to actually put her and Agar's skills to use.

Now that she and Agar had been under fire, she wasn't nearly as excited. More cautious, yes. A little frightened? She'd be a liar if she said she wasn't. Her next engagement with the enemy might be without the SEAL team as backup. She might not be as lucky without them.

She had to face it. T-Mac wouldn't be there every time she went outside the wire, and that made her sad.

Her chest tightened and her eyes burned. A single tear slipped from the corner of her eye, down her cheek.

She raised her free hand to brush away the moisture. Her drill sergeant in Basic Combat Training had assured her vehemently that soldiers didn't cry. Now wasn't a good time to start. Surrounded by SEALs who'd been through a whole lot more, she couldn't show any weakness.

Yet another damned tear slipped down the other cheek, closest to T-Mac.

He raised his hand as if to brush it away, but caught himself before he touched her. Instead, he pushed his hand through his hair and let it drop to his lap.

Kinsley had wanted him to touch her cheek. But she knew any public displays of affection were frowned upon and, in front of his buddies, would be purely awkward. So she sat still, hiding her disappointment, wishing she and T-Mac were alone again where they could hold each other, kiss and touch to their hearts' content.

Kinsley must have fallen asleep on the ride back. The change in the speed of the aircraft and the gentle squeeze on her hand brought her back to consciousness.

The chopper came down on the tarmac and the SEALs piled out.

Still a little groggy from her short nap, Kinsley took her time climbing down.

T-Mac stood on the ground, holding out his hand.

She stumbled and fell into his arms.

He caught her and held her briefly, perhaps hugging her harder than he would a stranger. Then he set her up straight and gathered Agar's lead from the ground where she'd dropped it. "Steady there," he whispered.

She nodded, her cheeks burning. "Thanks."

"We're all due to report to Commander Ward in the command center," Big Jake reminded them.

Kinsley nodded, all her grogginess wiped clean. They were back. Rules and regulations couldn't be ignored. She couldn't hold T-Mac's hand or steal a kiss whenever she liked. Tired, grungy and ready for a shower and a real bed, she squared her shoulders and marched alongside the SEALs, her hand wrapped around Agar's lead. The vacation was over.

Ha! Some vacation. They'd been shot at, nearly blown up and on the run for the past thirty-six hours. And somewhere in there had been the most magical point of her life. Making love with T-Mac had changed everything. Inside, her heart bubbled with the need to shout out how good he'd made her feel. How he'd lit a fire inside the woman in her. Couldn't everyone see that? T-Mac had made her feel so very different.

And she could do nothing about it.

Kinsley pushed her hair behind her ears and tried to tuck it into the back of her shirt. She'd long since lost the elastic band that held it off her face. Yet she would stand in front of the mission commander, in her dirty uniform, and tell him everything that had happened.

Except what she considered the most significant... what had happened between her and T-Mac.

If the truth got out, neither one of their careers would survive. Time to suck it up and be a professional. In order to do that, she'd have to cut all ties and forget what had happened between her and T-Mac.

Like that would ever happen.

Even if she'd never forget her night with the SEAL, she would have to pretend it never took place.

Somehow, she made it through the debrief. When she left the command center, T-Mac cornered her in the shadow of one of the buildings.

"Kinsley, I can't pretend what we have together means nothing. I don't want this to be the end."

Her heart pinching in her chest, Kinsley held up her hand and shook her head. "Don't."

He gripped her arms. "What do you mean?"

"We're on two divergent paths, heading in completely different directions. We are destined to be apart. The sooner we accept that, the better off we'll both be."

He held her arms for a moment longer. When footsteps sounded on the gravel, he dropped his hands. "Is that the way you want it?"

She nodded, her eyes stinging with unshed tears. "It is."

"Very well." He took a step back. "I'll let you have time to think about it. But I can tell you now… I don't give up that easily. I wouldn't have come as far as I have… I wouldn't have made it through SEAL training if I gave up on what I wanted." He leaned closer so only she could hear his next words. "And I want you, Kinsley Anderson. I. Want. You."

Chapter Fourteen

T-Mac walked away from Kinsley, his chest tight, his fists clenched. He wanted to turn and run right back to her and kiss her until she changed her mind. He knew, deep inside, that she wanted him as much as he wanted her. She couldn't have faked her response to him when he'd held her in his arms and made sweet love to her. And she couldn't have faked how much she enjoyed kissing him when they were waiting for the helicopter.

She was a rule follower, and the rules were firmly in place at Camp Lemonnier. Breaking them would get them in trouble, and T-Mac didn't want to jeopardize Kinsley's career. He'd pushed the limits, bent a few rules and done things that could have harmed his own career, but he couldn't sabotage Kinsley's. She loved working with Agar. He knew a dog handler might not always get to work with the same dog. Kinsley knew it, too. If she were reassigned or got off active duty, Agar would still belong to the army.

Until he was retired, he'd have to go back to work. With another handler.

If Kinsley got in sufficient trouble, she could be kicked out of the military or reassigned to a different skill set and no longer be allowed to train with the dogs.

T-Mac's strides ate the distance as he passed the motor pool. The acrid scent of something burning irritated his nose. A yell made him slow to a stop and glance around.

"Someone help!" a voice cried out. "Man down!"

T-Mac altered his direction and headed toward the sound—and a growing cloud of black smoke.

As he rounded the corner of the motor-pool building, he could see a young marine dragging another man in uniform across the pavement.

T-Mac ran toward them, grabbed one of the inert man's arms and helped the marine drag him out of the smoke.

Harm, Diesel, Pitbull, Big Jake and Buck appeared beside him.

Buck dove in. "Let me check for a pulse."

T-Mac moved aside while Buck put his medical training to good use. He pressed his fingers to the base of the man's throat and stared at his chest. "No pulse and he's not breathing." Immediately, Buck began compressions against the man's chest. "Breathe for him while I work on his pulse." He pointed at the young marine standing by. "You! Get help."

The marine sprinted toward the next building.

Soon they were surrounded by people. A fire truck arrived and an ambulance pulled up. The trained medics took over from Buck.

The firefighters went to work on the fire burning inside the building. The medics loaded the injured man into the back of the ambulance and whisked him away to the medical facility, leaving the rest to pick up, clean up and get on with their own work.

T-Mac found the marine who'd originally pulled the man out of the motor-pool building. "What happened?"

The young man shrugged. "I don't know. One minute, Jones was fine. I went to the base exchange to get us a candy bar, and when I got back, smoke was billowing out of the building. I ran in to find Jones on the floor. If you hadn't come along..." He shook his head, his cheeks smudged with soot. "Do you think he'll make it?"

Buck stood beside T-Mac. "We did all we could. It's up to the medics and the doctors now."

"I don't get it. What would have started that fire?" He stared at the building where the firefighters were winding up the hoses.

"You should head to the medical facility and have them check you out for smoke inhalation."

The marine squared his shoulders. "I'm fine. But I'll go check on Jones."

"Seriously, man." Buck touched the man's shoulder. "Smoke inhalation might not hit you immediately. Better safe than sorry."

"Okay. I'll check in with the doc." The marine left.

The SEALs stood staring at the wreckage of the motor-pool building.

"What are the chances," T-Mac mused, "that we find a vehicle from this motor pool in the hands of Al-Shabaab, and the next thing we know, the motor pool building and all its records are burned to the ground?"

Big Jake shook his head. "Too much of a coincidence."

T-Mac's jaw tightened. "I don't believe in coincidence."

"We still don't know who was after your little dog handler," Harm reminded him.

T-Mac turned away from the building. "You're right."

"Her dog should keep her safe," Diesel assured him.

"Yeah, but he can only do so much." T-Mac left his team and walked toward the containerized living units. His walk became a jog, and then he was sprinting toward the one assigned to Kinsley. When he arrived, he pounded on the door.

When he got no answer, he glanced around wildly. She wasn't anywhere to be seen. He pounded again. "Specialist Anderson!"

A female poked her head out of the unit beside Kinsley's and frowned. "Hey, you might want to keep it down. Some of us work nights."

"Do you know where Specialist Anderson is?" he asked.

"No, but she might be in the shower unit." When T-Mac turned in that direction, the woman added, "I wouldn't go barging in on her. They frown on that kind of thing, you know." She chuckled and closed the door.

"Looking for me?" a voice said behind T-Mac.

He turned to find Kinsley wearing her PT gear and shower shoes. She carried a shower caddie of toiletries and her hair was wound up, turban-style, in a towel. Agar stood at her side, his coat slick and damp.

T-Mac caught himself before he did something stupid, like grab her and pull her into his arms.

She frowned. "Is everything all right?"

He shook his head. "I'm not sure you're safe."

"Why? What happened?"

"There was an accident at the motor pool. A fire and a man knocked unconscious."

Her eyes rounded. "That's awful. Is he going to be okay?"

"I don't know." He explained his concern about the fire coming on the heels of finding the motor-pool truck in the Al-Shabaab camp.

"You think the fire and attack in the motor pool had something to do with the stolen truck?" She pulled the towel from her head, looped it over her shoulder and finger combed her hair.

"What do you think?" he asked, wishing he could run his hands through her wet hair.

"Sounds too coincidental to me." She glanced down at the ground. "Do you think someone is trying to destroy the record of who checked it out?"

"That's what I'm thinking."

"Are all records stored online now?" she asked.

"I'm pretty sure they are," T-Mac said. "But the fire could have destroyed the computer." He lifted his head. "And the data might be stored on a database at a remote server." T-Mac smiled. "I'll check on that."

"In the meantime," Kinsley nodded toward her quarters, "I have a date with a blow dryer."

"Okay then." He stepped aside.

As she passed, he touched her arm. "I'm still not giving up on us."

She sighed and stared at the fingers on her arm. "Do you know how hard it is not to throw myself into your arms?" she whispered. Her gaze rose to meet his. "Just leave me alone. I can't be this close to you and not touch you. It's killing me."

As it was killing him. He nodded. "Don't let your guard down for a minute. Whoever attacked the guy in the motor pool might still consider you a threat."

"I don't know why. It's not like I remember anything from the attack in that village." She pressed her lips together. "But I'll be careful. And Agar will be with me at all times."

"Good." He nodded toward her door. "Let Agar go in first."

She gave him a gentle smile. "I always do." Kinsley turned toward her unit and stopped. "For the unofficial record, I miss being out in the desert, just you and me."

"Then why won't you consider seeing me again?"

Kinsley smiled sadly. "Because it will make the parting even harder. We're both married to our careers."

He smiled. "Then I want a divorce."

"You can't. You and I both have a number of years to complete our obligations." She lifted her head and stared directly into his eyes. "We can't tell the army and navy to go take a hike just because we might want to be together."

"Why not?"

"Because of all the attributes we've identified we like about each other, including loyalty and patriotism."

"But I don't want to give up on you...on us," he said, and reached out for her hand.

She stepped back and glanced right and left. "We can't be together, and it would be foolish to think otherwise. Long-distance relationships rarely work."

"I'm willing to give it a try."

"I'm not willing to hold you to it."

T-Mac pounded his fist into his palm. "Damn it, Kinsley, why do you have to be so obstinate and... and..." He sighed. "Most likely right."

She smiled, her eyes glistening with what he suspected were unshed tears. "Give it time. You'll forget Djibouti ever happened."

"Nope. Not a possibility. I don't want to forget it, and I suspect you don't either."

"For now, respect my decision," she said, and looked up at him, a tear slipping from the corner of her eye. "Leave me alone."

He inhaled a long, deep breath to calm his hammering heart. Then he let it out. "Okay. For now. But this isn't over. I won't let it be."

"I'm sorry," she said. "It has to be." Then she ducked past him and entered her unit with Agar, shutting the door behind them.

ONCE THE DOOR was closed behind Agar, Kinsley let the tears fall unchecked. She threw herself onto her bunk and hugged her pillow to her face to muffle the sobs. She wanted to be with T-Mac more than she wanted to breathe. But they couldn't abandon their careers. They each had a commitment to uphold. She had three more years on her current enlistment. In three years, they could each find someone else. Someone who wasn't so far away.

Yet Kinsley was certain she wouldn't find anyone she cared about as much as she'd learned to care about T-Mac in the few short days she'd known him. But he had an important job to do. He needed all his focus to be on staying alive and accomplishing his assigned dangerous missions. Trying to work out the logistics of a long-distance relationship would only make him lose focus. And that could be deadly.

After a good cry, she dried her tears, pulled back

her hair, dressed in her uniform and went to the chow hall for dinner. She hoped she wouldn't run into anyone from T-Mac's SEAL team. Agar trotted along at her side.

In the dining facility, she collected a tray of food, not really hungry but knowing she had to keep up her strength should she and Agar be assigned to another mission. At the very least, she might be put back on gate-guard rotation. At that moment, she'd almost prefer the monotony of guarding the entrance of the camp. At least then she wouldn't run the risk of bumping into T-Mac.

Her gaze drifted to the door more often than she cared to admit. Part of her wanted T-Mac to walk through. Another part prayed he wouldn't.

"Mind if I sit with you?" a voice said, drawing her attention away from the entrance.

She looked up to find Mr. Toland hovering over her, holding a tray of food. Kinsley shrugged. "Not at all," she said, though she'd rather be alone with her thoughts. But she didn't want to be rude to the contractor.

"I hear you and one of the navy SEALs have been on quite the adventure."

Using her fork, she stabbed the meat on her platter and cut it with a knife. "If you want to call it that," she replied.

"We all thought you and the SEAL were casualties when you didn't make it back with the others."

"We weren't," she said, stating the obvious.

"I was surprised they sent you out again after your last mission resulted in a concussion."

Tired of the man's conversation, Kinsley turned to him and gave him a direct stare. "I'm sorry, sir, but information about missions is classified. I'm not allowed to discuss the details."

He held up his hands. "Of course. I wouldn't want you to get into trouble."

Good. Then maybe you can go away. She wanted to say the words, but she refused to take out her bad temper on the contractor.

"I was just worried about you. You remind me of my daughter." He smiled. "How are you feeling after the concussion?"

Feeling a little guilty for jumping down the man's throat, Kinsley answered, "Perfectly fine, except for a little memory loss."

"Really?" Mr. Toland nodded. "Sometimes situationally induced concussions can result in memory loss. You don't remember anything before the blow that knocked you unconscious?"

She frowned hard, trying to force the memories out. Finally, she shook her head. "Nothing." *But I feel like I'm forgetting something really important.* She stared into the man's eyes. "You know, like it's right there on the edge of my memory, just waiting to come back." She laughed. "Maybe I just need another knock in the head for it to shake loose." Kinsley shrugged. "At least I didn't forget how to work with Agar or how to hold my fork." She lifted her utensil as proof.

"Strange thing, the brain," Mr. Toland said. "I've heard of people never recalling tragic events. Then I've heard of people suddenly remembering all of it."

"You never know with amnesia." Kinsley wished she could forget how much she cared for T-Mac. Then again, she didn't want to forget, because he was such an important part of her life. He'd shown her how real her emotions could be and how much she wanted that in her life.

She stared down at her tray, giving up on refueling her body. "If you'll excuse me, I think I'll go for a run." She stowed her tray, gathered Agar's lead in her hand and left the dining facility.

The only way she could clear her mind was to run until she was too tired to think. Even then, she doubted she'd forget T-Mac. Most likely, he'd haunt her dreams for years to come.

Outside, she hurried back to her quarters and slipped out of her uniform and into her PT clothes. Agar danced around her, knowing he would be included on her run. The dog needed to blow off steam as much as Kinsley. A run around the perimeter would be just what they both needed.

When she stepped out of her quarters and started for the field beyond, she spotted T-Mac jogging ahead of her.

She almost turned around and went back into her container to hide.

Agar tugged on his lead, eager to get out and run.

Kinsley couldn't disappoint the animal. He needed the exercise, and she had to get used to seeing T-Mac in passing until they left to return to the States. Hadn't his commander said something about them redeploying in four days? That had been a few days before. If they were still on track to return to Virginia, they'd be leaving soon.

Good. At least then she could start down the road to recovery. In the meantime, she jogged behind T-Mac, admiring the way his muscles bunched and how graceful he was when he ran.

Her imagination took her back to when they were lying naked on the front seat of the truck. His buttocks were hard and tight beneath her fingertips.

Her heart beat faster and her breathing became more labored than her slow, steady pace warranted.

When he turned at the far end of the field and circled back toward the living quarters, he spied her. For a moment, he slowed, his brows dipping into a fierce frown.

Kinsley focused on putting one foot in front of the other, if a little slower. She prayed he wouldn't stop and wait, or run back to her. She wasn't sure she could keep up her adamant refusal to see him again, when all she really wanted was to be with him always.

How did this happen? How did she fall for a military guy after losing her first love? She knew the dangers of death and separation.

Thankfully, T-Mac kept running toward their quarters without slowing significantly. As he neared the living area, five of his teammates met him. They put their heads together and spoke in low tones. Whatever they were saying didn't carry on the wind.

Having been a part of their mission task force, Kinsley was interested in what was going on. She might have input into the next operation, and she sure as hell wanted to know if they'd followed the GPS tracking device to where the Al-Shabaab rebels had moved.

Kinsley picked up the pace, racing to the group of men, Agar running easily alongside.

"Hey, Specialist Anderson." Big Jake held out a hand.

Kinsley came to an abrupt stop and took Big Jake's hand in a firm shake. "What's going on?"

"Got word back from the doc at the medical center," Buck said, his lips forming a thin line. "The guy from the motor pool didn't make it."

"Smoke inhalation?" Kinsley guessed.

Buck shook his head. "Blunt force trauma to the back of his skull. We couldn't have saved him."

Kinsley's chest tightened. "Why?"

"Either he knew something or he got in the way of someone burning the building is my guess," Big Jake said.

"The weapons, the truck, they're all part of whatever is going on here at Camp Lemonnier." Kinsley frowned, pushing hard to remember. "I get the feeling I should know something or that I saw something that night I was shot in the chest." She smacked her forehead, angry at her inability to pull those few minutes of her life, seemingly lost. "If only I could remember."

"Don't worry about it," Harm said. "It's probably your mind's way of protecting you. It had to be pretty horrific to see a gun pointed at your chest and not be able to do anything to stop the shooter from pulling the trigger."

"Still…" She sighed. "If only I were a computer with a reboot button."

"On the bright side," Big Jake interjected, "the commander had the UAV team track the GPS you two planted on the Al-Shabaab truck." He paused dramatically.

"And?" T-Mac questioned impatiently.

"The truck led them to their new camp." Big Jake's eyes narrowed. "Once they determined there were no civilians in the way, the UAV team dropped missiles in their midst. They won't be using our weapons and vehicles against us anytime soon."

Kinsley crossed her arms over her chest and her eyes narrowed. "Good riddance. But what happened to capturing one of them to determine who their supplier is?"

"That decision wasn't ours to make," Big Jake said. "The commander decided it wasn't worth risking the lives of our SEALs and dog handler again."

"And we're still due to redeploy back to home base

tomorrow," T-Mac said. His gaze captured hers. "Our transport leaves at seven in the morning."

Kinsley's heart plummeted to the pit of her belly, and her knees wobbled. She'd known they would leave soon, but she'd selfishly hoped they would be delayed a few more days. "What about the supplier connection? Isn't Commander Ward concerned about finding the link?"

"He is, but he's bringing in an investigator and working with the intel guys looking into the motor-pool database. He thinks they'll be able to trace back to the man responsible. And since we were able to bring the weapons back, they might be able to pull a serial number and find out who shipped them in the first place."

"So you're done here?" She smiled, though her heart hurt so badly she could barely breathe. "I know you'll be glad to get back home."

"Some of us will be happier than others," Harm said, his eyes sliding sideways, aiming toward T-Mac. "We'd better go pack our gear." He gave a chin lift to the others. "And leave T-Mac to fill in Specialist Anderson on anything we might have left out."

"What did we leave out?" Pitbull asked.

Harm glared at the man and jerked his head toward T-Mac and Kinsley. "I'm sure we've left off something. T-Mac will fill her in." He gave Pitbull a shove. "Sometimes you can be so thickheaded."

"Oh." Pitbull grinned. "You want to let T-Mac

have some time alone with his dog handler. Why didn't you say so in the first place?"

Harm raised his face to the heavens. "I'm surrounded by morons."

"Watch it, dude." Pitbull shoved Harm. "I have feelings."

The five SEALs left T-Mac alone with Kinsley.

"I hope you have a good flight back to the States." Kinsley refused to look into T-Mac's eyes. Hers were burning with unshed tears, and if she didn't get away soon, she'd lose it in front of him. "Safe travels," she said, her voice catching. Then she turned and would have run but for the hand that grabbed her elbow and held on.

"I want to see you again."

"No," she whispered, staring down at the hand on her arm. "It's better to end it now than to drag it out."

"Will you be there in the morning when we take off?"

"No." She shook her head. "I have to be on duty at the gate," she lied. Since she'd been tasked to aid the SEAL missions, she hadn't been added back to the gate-inspection schedule. But she couldn't let T-Mac see her standing by, watching them leave. She'd be all red faced and tear streaked. And if she didn't get away from him quickly, she'd be that way all too soon. "I have to go." She ducked past him and ran.

Kinsley had marched right into enemy territory, stood face to face with a killer who had shot her in the chest and fought terrorists from a moving vehicle, but she ran from T-Mac because she was afraid.

She was afraid of losing someone she loved. Again. Maybe her reasoning for running didn't make sense, but she had to get away. He was leaving. She was staying. By the time she returned to the States, he'd be off on his next mission or—worse yet—on to his next girlfriend.

Not that Kinsley was ever his girlfriend. Knowing each other for such a short time shouldn't have made her feel this strongly about T-Mac. But there she was, crying like a baby, her vision blurring so much she ran into someone.

Hands reached out to steady her. "Specialist Anderson, are you all right?"

"I'm fine," she said, and then sniffed loudly and blinked enough to clear her eyes and look up at Mr. Toland. "I'm sorry. I'm just…just… They're leaving in the morning," she cried, and the tears fell faster.

"The navy SEALs?" he asked.

"Yes."

"Things always have a way of working out," he said.

She rubbed her hand over her face, knowing her situation with T-Mac would never work and talking it over with a stranger wouldn't make her feel any better. "I'm sorry. I need to go."

With Agar at her side, Kinsley ran all the way back to her quarters, pushed through the door and collapsed on her small cot. She cried herself to sleep, wishing there was another way.

She'd be up early to watch their plane take off, despite telling him she wouldn't.

Chapter Fifteen

Pounding on the door to the unit T-Mac and Harm shared startled T-Mac awake. He glanced at the clock. Two in the morning. "What the heck?"

"Seriously." Harm swung his legs out of his bunk.

"Wake up, T-Mac!" Big Jake called out from the other side of the door. "We've got orders to move out."

T-Mac pushed the door open. "Thought we weren't leaving until seven."

"Plans changed," Big Jake said. "We have one more operation before we bug out. Gear up. We leave in fifteen."

All sleepiness disappeared in seconds. T-Mac grabbed his go bag and upended it onto his bunk. He jammed his legs into dark pants and boots, pulled a dark T-shirt over his head and slipped a black jacket over his shoulders. He knew the drill, knew exactly what he needed, and in under five minutes he was fully dressed, wearing his body armor vest and carrying enough weapons and ammunition to start his

own damned war. He settled his helmet, complete
with his night-vision goggles, on his head and slung
his M4A1 rifle strap over his shoulder.

Harm finished preparing at the same time.

Together they left the unit and headed for the landing strip, where the helicopters sat with rotor blades
turning.

Big Jake, Diesel, Pitbull and Buck were climbing
aboard when T-Mac and Harm arrived.

T-Mac hopped on board only to find one more
person already there with her dog.

He grinned, happier to see her than he could say
out loud. He settled his headset over his ears and
waited for the others to do the same.

All the while, he couldn't stop staring at Kinsley where she sat beside him. He reached out and
scratched Agar behind the ears.

"Comm check," Big Jake said into his mic.

They went around the interior of the helicopter
calling out their names.

"You all might be wondering why we were called
out without any warning," Jake started as the rotor
blades spun faster and louder.

Everyone nodded.

"Commander Ward received a message from intel
that our attack yesterday did not take out the leader
of the Al-Shabaab rebels. They were able to locate
his position. We have the new coordinates and are
tasked with taking him out. If this mission goes well,

we'll be back in time to ship out. Maybe not at seven in the morning, but at least by noon."

"Good. Marly's supposed to get back from her chartered flight tomorrow," Pitbull said. "She promised not to fly any more gigs until we've had time to really see each other." He patted his flat belly. "And I have a steak with my name on it back at the steakhouse in Little Creek."

"I can't wait to see Reese," Diesel said. "We're finally going out on an honest-to-goodness date. I'm not sure how to act."

"Talia has been busy redecorating my apartment. I can't wait to test out the new king-size bed," Harm said.

"Angela's been too busy at the hospital to care about the furniture in my apartment," Buck said. "I imagine we'll find a house pretty quickly."

"I can't wait to see Alex." Big Jake smiled. "She should be settled into her new teaching job."

Everyone had someone to go home to back in the States. Everyone but T-Mac. He had everything he wanted in the helicopter at that moment. If he could, he'd extend his stay in Djibouti just to be with Kinsley. This extra mission meant he got to see her one more time. He might even get to hold her hand as they flew to their location.

The Black Hawk lifted off the tarmac and rose into the star-studded night sky.

Moments later they were high above the ground.

They headed out over the Gulf of Aden and started to turn south.

A loud bang sounded over the noise-reducing headsets. The helicopter shook violently, and shrapnel pierced the shell.

Kinsley yelped and doubled over, grabbing for T-Mac's hand.

The motor shut down and the helicopter fell from the sky.

Over the headset, the pilot's tense voice sounded. "Brace for landing."

As the chopper lost altitude, T-Mac reached his free hand for the buckles on the harness holding him in his seat. They would have only seconds after hitting the water to get out. If the helicopter rolled upside down, the confusion of which way was up and which was down in the dark would be deadly.

He and his teammates had gone through special training on how to get out of a helicopter that had gone down in the water. They knew how to get out. He'd bet Kinsley had not had similar training.

Based on the way she squeezed his hand, she was scared. Her fear was about to multiply.

Right before the chopper hit the water, it tilted, slowed and then slammed into it. As soon as they hit, buckles popped free and SEALs pushed away from their seats.

T-Mac ripped open his seat-harness buckles and floated free.

The helicopter rolled and filled with water so fast,

T-Mac barely had time to pull his arms free of the harness. He let go of Kinsley's hand only for a moment, but that moment was too long. He held his breath, his lungs burning, hands reaching in the darkness, searching for Kinsley.

The arms and legs of his teammates floated against him as they struggled to find their way out through the open doors.

Just when T-Mac's lungs felt as if they would burst, a small hand wrapped around his wrist.

T-Mac grabbed Kinsley's arm and pulled her out of the helicopter and swam for the surface, his own buoyancy leading him in the right direction. A moment later, his head breached and he gulped in air.

Kinsley's head popped up beside him. She coughed and sputtered, dragging in huge breaths. As soon as she stopped coughing, she yelled, "Agar!"

Splashing sounded beside them and Agar dog-paddled over to Kinsley, whining pitifully. T-Mac swam toward them.

"Head count and status!" Big Jake's voice boomed across the water. "Buck."

"Alive and bleeding," Buck called out.

"Pitbull," Big Jake yelled.

"Here," Pitbull answered. "Nothing but a goose egg on my forehead from where Diesel kicked me."

"Harm." Big Jake sputtered and coughed.

"Took some shrapnel to my thigh," Harm said. "But I'm alive. Hurts like hell."

"T-Mac and Specialist Anderson?" Big Jake queried.

"We made it. And Agar's here." T-Mac continued to hold on to Kinsley's hand. If anyone wanted him to let go, they'd have to pry his cold dead fingers loose. He wasn't letting go of her ever again. She treaded water with her free hand but clung to him like a lifeline.

"Commander Ward?" Big Jake called out.

A moment went by.

"Commander?" Big Jake repeated.

"I'm here," he said, his voice weak. "I think my arm is broken."

"Gotcha, sir." Buck swam over to the older man and helped him stay above water.

"What about the pilot and copilot?" Big Jake called out.

"Pilot here. We both made it out, but the Black Hawk is toast."

"What happened?" Big Jake swam up to T-Mac and treaded water.

"Didn't you feel it?" the pilot said. "Someone shot us down."

T-Mac's grip tightened on Kinsley's hand. "That's what it felt like."

"Who the hell would shoot us down from Djibouti?" Harm asked.

"Al-Shabaab?"

"Or whoever is supplying them." T-Mac's jaw

tightened as he struggled to tread water with one hand.

"Oh, hell." Kinsley rubbed her forehead with her free hand while kicking her feet to keep her face above the surface.

"What's wrong? Besides being in deep water with no life raft?" T-Mac held on to her, helping to keep her afloat.

"My knee hurts like hell, for one," she said. "And I hit my head coming out of the chopper."

"Are you feeling dizzy? Confused?" Buck swam over to where she bobbed in the water.

T-Mac wished he could get her out of the water and to the nearest medical facility. But they'd have to wait until folks at Camp Lemonnier realized what had happened. "It won't be long. They had to have seen the explosion. We'll get you the help you need."

"No. You don't understand." She pressed her palm to the top of her head. "I… I…remember!" She glanced up and stared across at T-Mac.

"Everything?" T-Mac asked, his heart swelling.

She nodded and struggled to tread water. "Everything."

WHEN THE CHOPPER had gone down, Kinsley had braced for the landing. She knew the dangers of landing in the water and had her hands on her seat belt before they crashed into the Gulf of Aden. She'd released her harness a fraction of a second too soon. When they hit, she flew out of the harness and slammed her head against the top of the fuselage, and twisted her leg so hard she'd felt something snap in her knee, accompanied by a sharp stab of pain. She'd seen stars and feared she'd pass out. But all she could think about were T-Mac and Agar. She had to get out to save them.

The knock on her head made her disoriented. When the chopper rolled in the waves, Kinsley went under. Like a movie playing at high speed, her memories flashed through her mind, all the way up to, and including, the current crash. She'd seen her first meeting with T-Mac, the time he had thrown himself into her quarters to protect her from an unexploded package. He'd been so darned sexy.

Memories of her first night out chasing down enemies hung in the background. She remembered leading the SEAL team with Agar. They'd found numerous land mines through the rubble of the little village, Agar doing his thing, following his nose.

Kinsley remembered her jolt of fear when Agar entered that hut. She'd turned the corner and charged into the building before she thought through the consequences.

And then she'd shone her light into the face of someone she recognized. "The man who shot me. I remember who it was!" she said, and dipped below the surface, choking on a mouthful of salt water.

T-Mac jerked her back to the surface. "Breathe," he said. "We'll worry about who it was when we're out of the water."

"But I know who it was. It was that contractor working on the improvements to the camp."

"Which contractor?" the commander asked.

"Toland. William Toland." A gate opened in Kinsley's mind and all the memories flooded in. She pushed through the pain in her knee, relying on one leg and her arms to keep her head above water.

The roar of rotor blades sounded, coming from the direction of Camp Lemonnier.

Joyful relief filled Kinsley. Not only would they survive a crash, she remembered who'd shot her.

"Toland has to be the one responsible for the gun trading and the information leaks," T-Mac said. "Wasn't he involved in renovating the command center?"

"He was," Commander Ward said. "He could have bugged the room with electronic devices."

"Look, when we're taken back to the camp, let everyone believe Specialist Anderson didn't make it. We'll have her delivered directly to the medical facility, but have the doctors announce that she's dead."

"Why?"

"We want Toland to think he's in the clear," Harm said. "The only eyewitness to him being in that Al-Shabaab camp will be dead. He might get careless. At the very least, we'll be able to catch him before he tries to make a run for it."

"Are you game to play dead?" T-Mac asked Kinsley.

"I'd rather be in on the action. That man tried to kill me." She treaded water for a few seconds before adding, "But I have to be realistic. Something's wrong with my knee. I'll play dead, but you have to promise me you'll get him."

"Are you sure it was him?" Harm asked.

"Absolutely," Kinsley said, her arm getting weaker as her strength waned. "I remember seeing his shock of gray hair before he pulled the trigger." Her eyes narrowed. Yeah, she'd like to be there at his takedown. He'd tried to kill her.

"We'll take care of him," T-Mac said, his face dark and hardened into stone.

When the Black Hawk arrived, Kinsley and Agar went up first on the hoist as the chopper hovered over the water. One by one, the rest of the men were reeled in. Buck stabilized her leg by applying a temporary splint. The pain was so bad, Kinsley passed out several times en route back to land.

By the time they returned to camp, it was late. Nevertheless, Kinsley was loaded onto a stretcher and into an ambulance to be delivered to the medical facility. She was sequestered in a room at the back of the building, along with Agar. No one was allowed to enter but the doctor and Commander Ward. The doctor suspected she'd torn her ACL or her meniscus. They'd have to send her back to the States to have an MRI. Fortunately, a C-130 airplane was scheduled to leave the next day. She would be on it. They discussed the plan to declare her dead. The doctor set her up with an IV and pain meds before leaving her and Agar alone.

The commander called in the veterinarian to perform a house call and check Agar over. The dog had been limping so badly, he'd been brought into the medical facility on a stretcher as well. He lay on a bed that had been pushed up to the side of Kinsley's.

When the veterinarian came, he gave Agar pain meds and recommended he be airlifted out along with Kinsley and taken to a veterinarian surgical clinic, where they would have the equipment to better treat the animal.

Kinsley couldn't tell how much time had passed. She floated in and out of a cloud of pain, the morphine the doctor had given her barely taking the edge off.

Kinsley lay on the hospital bed and waited for someone to come tell her that Toland had been captured and locked in the brig. At the very least, she wanted to shower the salt water off her skin. A nurse had helped her out of her uniform and into a hospital gown under strict instructions to keep quiet about Kinsley being alive.

Alone in the hospital bed with Agar in drug-induced sleep, whining every time he moved, Kinsley could only imagine what was happening. Every scenario she came up with ended badly. When she heard footsteps in the hallway, she held her breath and prayed it was T-Mac coming to tell her they'd caught Toland.

The pain medication finally took its toll and claimed Kinsley in sleep.

THE GRAY LIGHT of morning edged its way around the shades over the window when Kinsley opened her eyes.

She stared up at the ceiling for a moment, trying to remember where she was and what had happened. Her skin felt sticky, and that's when she recalled all that had happened the night before and all that she'd forgotten from when she'd been shot. She turned her head to see dark red hair lying on the sheet beside her, a big hand holding hers in its grip.

"T-Mac," she whispered, and reached over to smooth her hand through his auburn hair. It wouldn't be so bad to have red-haired children. As long as they looked like the navy SEAL who'd stolen her heart.

He raised his head and stared into her eyes. "Hey, beautiful."

She snorted softly. "Hardly. I'm sure I look like I've been dunked in the ocean and put up wet."

"Which is beautiful to me."

"Did they get Toland?"

"They did. And he confessed to trading the weapons. He was also working with a guy in the motor pool to transport the goods."

"The guy who died?" Kinsley asked.

T-Mac nodded. "Toland killed him to shut him up."

"He admitted to the murder?"

His brows dipping lower, T-Mac pressed his lips together in a tight line. "Toland was more afraid of us than of going to jail. He spilled his guts."

Kinsley sighed. "Good. He'll get what he deserves. The man is a traitor."

"Yes, he is." He leaned across her and pressed his lips to hers. "But all that is done. How are you feeling?"

"Better, now that you're here." She wrapped her arms around his neck and pulled him down to return that kiss with all of her heart.

When they broke away for air, she smiled up at him. "Aren't you afraid we'll get in trouble?"

"I don't really care."

She chuckled. "Me either."

"They should be in soon to load you up into the plane and take you back to the States."

She touched his cheek. "I don't want this to end."

He cupped her hand and pressed a kiss to her palm. "Me either."

"It might not have to." She glanced down at her leg. "I might be medically boarded out."

"The doc thinks you tore your ACL or meniscus."

She nodded.

"And if they medically retire you?" T-Mac looked at her. "What then?"

Her hand slid across the sheet to smooth over Agar's head. The dog whined and tried to lick her fingers.

"I'll probably go on and get that college degree I

joined the military for." She met his gaze with a direct one of her own. "If Agar is retired as well, I want to give him a forever home with a yard to run in."

"There are some great colleges in Virginia," T-Mac offered.

"Yeah?" Kinsley smiled, tears welling in her eyes. "Will you want to date a gimpy girl?"

"I'll want you no matter what, my sweet, brave dog handler." He slid onto the bed beside her and carefully gathered her into his arms. "You're amazing, and I want to spend a lot more time getting to know you. Like the rest of my life. Baby, you're the one."

She shook her head. "How do you know I'm the one? We haven't known each other very long."

"A wise old friend of mine told me you don't have to know a person very long to know she's the one for you." He pushed a strand of her hair out of her face. "I didn't believe him, until I met the one person who convinced me."

"And who was that?" Kinsley whispered.

"I think you know."

"Hmm. Maybe I do. You better kiss me before my chariot arrives to take me away. This kiss will have to last me until I see you again." She brushed her lips across his. "Because when you know he's the right one, you just know."

Epilogue

Three months later...

"Need help bringing out that platter of marinated steaks?" T-Mac called out.

"No, I can manage." Kinsley limped out to the patio of the house they'd purchased together in the Little Creek area.

T-Mac smiled at her, his heart so full he couldn't believe how lucky he was to have found the love of his life.

"The gang will be here any minute. Should I put the steaks on right now, or wait to make sure they arrive on time?"

"Wait. The guys like them practically raw." She set the tray of steaks next to the grill.

T-Mac captured her around the waist and pulled her into his arms, kissing her soundly. "I'm the lucki-est man alive."

"Oh, yeah, how's that?" She leaned back against his arms around her middle and smiled up at him.

"I have you, don't I?"

"That makes me the luckiest woman alive."

"Even though you had to give up the army?" He kissed the tip of her nose. "Do you miss it?"

She shrugged. "I do miss helping keep our guys safe. But since Agar and I were both injured and retired, it worked out for the best. I can be around to see to Agar's needs, and you and I get to be together."

A damp nose pushed between T-Mac and Kinsley's legs.

"That's right, Agar. You're loved, too." Kinsley reached down and patted the dog's head.

He would walk with a limp for the rest of his life, but he was retired from active duty and would lead the good life with a big backyard to run in and a soft bed to sleep on.

"Hello! Anyone home?" a voice called out. "The gang's all here." Big Jake stepped through the patio doors with Alexandria Parker at his side.

Behind them were Buck and the love of his life, Dr. Angela Vega.

Diesel came out on the patio with Reese Brantley, the former army bodyguard with the fiery auburn hair and mad fighting skills that served her well in her chosen profession.

Pitbull held hands with Marly Simpson, the bush pilot he'd fallen in love with during a vacation in Africa. She'd relocated to the States and was flying for a charter company.

Harm followed Talia Ryan, the former owner of an African resort.

Talia carried a bottle of wine. "I hope you like red. I thought it would go well with the steak."

Kinsley smiled and took the offering. "I'll save it for later."

T-Mac circled her waist with his arms and grinned at Harm. "Nine months later."

"What?" Harm's jaw dropped. "Nine months? Are you saying what I think you're saying?"

"No kidding?" Buck grinned. "Kinsley's got a bun in the oven?"

Angela frowned. "Do people really say that anymore?" She hugged Kinsley. "I'm so happy for you two."

"When's the wedding?" Big Jake asked. "You have to make an honest woman of her now."

"Next weekend. If you all can make it," T-Mac announced.

"Oh, wow!" Marly exclaimed. "That's great. I'm pretty sure I don't have anything on my schedule that can't be pushed off."

"Where's it going to be?" Talia asked.

Kinsley laughed. "We're having a JP perform the ceremony on Virginia Beach. Someplace Agar can be a part of the ceremony."

"Do you need help with the preparations?" Alexandria asked. "I'm really good with decorations and flower arrangements."

"I'd love some help."

"Have you bought your wedding gown?" Talia asked.

Kinsley's cheeks flushed pink. "No, I haven't."

"Oh, sweetie, we have to get on that," Talia said. "I can help you there. How many bridesmaids and groomsmen?"

"None," T-Mac said. "It's just going to be Kinsley, me, Agar and all of our friends."

"Oh, and your parents and sister are coming," Kinsley added.

"What?" T-Mac frowned. "I haven't even told them I'm getting married."

"They know," she said, her face smug. "And they're so delighted you wanted them here to celebrate."

He laughed and pulled her into his arms. "You are the right one for me. Are they happy about their new grandson?"

"I'll let you share that news with them after the wedding." Kinsley lifted her chin. "But I'm sure they'll be ecstatic about their granddaughter."

Reese laughed. "Too early to know whether you're having a girl or boy?"

T-Mac nodded. "Yeah, and we won't until the baby's born."

"Oh, that's not fair. We want to know what it is," Buck complained.

"And you will." T-Mac said. "When the baby comes."

Harm shook his head. "I can't believe you're getting married before the rest of us." He pulled Talia into the circle of his arms. "I just got Talia to agree to marry me."

"Seriously?" T-Mac shook his friend's hand and

then hugged his fiancée. "I'm really happy for you two." He turned to Talia. "You're getting a great guy."

"I know." She smiled up into Harm's eyes. "He's been patient with me through my move back to the States. I wasn't sure I wanted to get married again. I loved my first husband so much. But I've learned I can love again, and Harm's the man who showed me how."

The others all gathered around to congratulate Harm and Talia, T-Mac and Kinsley.

"Anyone else holding out on us?" T-Mac asked. "Speak now before I put the steaks on the grill."

"Alex got a job teaching at the elementary school around the corner from our apartment," Jake said. "The kids all love her. And so do I." He hugged Alex and gave her a big kiss.

"I have an announcement," Buck said.

"That you're getting off active duty and going back to medical school?" Diesel guessed.

Buck frowned. "Hey, I was supposed to say that. How did you know? But yes, I was accepted into medical school. I start next spring."

Diesel opened the cooler he'd brought with him and tossed Buck a can of beer. "It's about damned time. You're going to make a great doctor. You and Angela can open your own practice when you're done."

"Anyone else?" T-Mac asked.

"I'm giving up my gig as a bodyguard," Reese announced.

Diesel frowned. "That's news to me. I thought you liked it."

"I did, but it's not really conducive to pregnant women." A smile spread across Reese's face.

"Pregnant?" Diesel's face went from shocked to joyous. "Are you kidding?" He lifted her off the ground and spun her around. "Really?" He lowered her to her feet and stared down into her eyes. "Sweetheart, I love you so much." He dropped to his knee and held her hand in his. "Will you marry me?"

Reese laughed. "You don't have to ask me if you don't want to marry me. I like things the way they are now. Why ruin it by getting married?"

Diesel straightened and gathered Reese in his arms. "Because I love you and would be honored if you'd be my partner, my lover and my friend in marriage."

"To love, honor and swing from tree to tree?" Pitbull joked.

"I'd do it, if she said *yes*," Diesel said, his gaze never leaving Reese's. "Will you marry me, Reese Brantley?"

She smiled up at him and nodded. "I will."

"Next week? Can we make it a double wedding on the beach?"

Reese gave T-Mac and Kinsley a nervous smile. "They might want to have a wedding all to themselves. I don't want to butt in."

"The more the merrier," T-Mac said.

"It's a great idea," Kinsley agreed. "And our babies will grow up together. How wonderful."

"Well, damn," Pitbull said. "We're not keeping up

with the rest of them." He started to bend down on one knee, but Marly beat him to it.

Marly held up her hand. "Before you start, let me say something."

Pitbull frowned.

"Will you marry me?" she asked, and grinned. "Beat you to it."

"Damn woman. Is this how it's going to be?" He pulled her into his arms and kissed her on the lips. "Because if it is, I'm in. Yes. I will."

More congratulations were offered.

T-Mac finally got the steaks on the grill, and he stood back with an arm around Kinsley, Agar lying at their feet and surrounded by the men and women who were so much a part of his life, they were like family.

"I'm truly the luckiest man alive," he said.

Kinsley leaned into him and smiled. "I love you, Trace McGuire. I'm glad you didn't give up on me."

* * * * *

Audrey Anderson will do whatever it takes to keep her family's newspaper running. Following a murder in town, Audrey must break the story, despite the fact that doing so will put her at risk. Can Sheriff Colt Tanner keep her out of trouble—or will their reignited love cause them to face even more danger?

Read on for a sneak preview of In Self Defense, *a thrilling new romantic suspense novel from* USA TODAY *bestselling author Debra Webb.*

Franklin County, Tennessee
Monday, February 25, 9:10 p.m.

The red-and-blue lights flashed in the night.

Audrey Anderson opened her car door and stepped out onto the gravel road. She grimaced and wished she'd taken time to change her shoes, but time was not an available luxury when the police scanner spit out the code for a shooting that ended in a call to the coroner. Good thing her dedicated editor, Brian Peterson, had his ear to the police radio pretty much 24/7 and immediately texted her.

The sheriff's truck was already on-site, along with two county cruisers and the coroner's van. So far no news vans and no cars that she noticed belonging to other reporters from the tri-county area. Strange, that cocky reporter from the *Tullahoma Telegraph* almost always arrived on the scene before Audrey. Maybe she had a friend in the department.

Then again, Audrey had her own sources, too. She reached back into the car for her bag. So far the closest private source she had was the sheriff himself—which was only because he still felt guilty for cheating on her back in high school.

Audrey was not above using that guilt whenever the need arose.

Tonight seemed like the perfect time to remind the man she'd once thought she would marry that he owed her one or two or a hundred.

She shuddered as the cold night air sent a shiver through her. Late February was marked by all sorts of lovely blooms and promises of spring, but it was all just an illusion. It was still winter and Mother Nature loved letting folks know who was boss. Like tonight—the gorgeous sixty-two-degree sunny day had turned into a bone-chilling evening. Audrey shivered, wishing she'd worn a coat to dinner.

Buncombe Road snaked through a farming community situated about halfway between Huntland and Winchester—every agricultural mile fell under the Franklin County sheriff's jurisdiction. The houses, mostly farmhouses sitting amid dozens if not hundreds of acres of pastures and fields, were scattered few and far between. But that wasn't the surprising part of the location. This particular house and farm belonged to a Mennonite family. Rarely did violence or any other sort of trouble within this quiet, closed community ripple beyond its boundaries. Most issues were handled privately and silently. The Mennonites kept to themselves for the most part and never bothered anyone. A few operated public businesses within the local community, and most interactions were kept strictly within the business domain. There was no real intermingling or socializing within the larger community—not even Winchester, which was the county seat and buzzed with activity.

Whatever happened inside this turn-of-the-nineteenth-century farmhouse tonight was beyond the closed community's ability to settle amid their own ranks.

Don't miss
In Self Defense *by Debra Webb,*
available February 2019 wherever
Harlequin® Intrigue books and ebooks are sold.

www.Harlequin.com

Need an adrenaline rush from nail-biting tales
(and irresistible males)?

Check out **Harlequin Intrigue®**,
Harlequin® Romantic Suspense and
Love Inspired® Suspense books!

New books available every month!

CONNECT WITH US AT:

Facebook.com/groups/HarlequinConnection

 Facebook.com/HarlequinBooks

 Twitter.com/HarlequinBooks

 Instagram.com/HarlequinBooks

Pinterest.com/HarlequinBooks

ReaderService.com

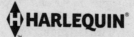

**ROMANCE WHEN
YOU NEED IT**

Love Harlequin romance?

DISCOVER.

Be the first to find out about promotions, news and exclusive content!

 Facebook.com/HarlequinBooks

Twitter.com/HarlequinBooks

Instagram.com/HarlequinBooks

Pinterest.com/HarlequinBooks

ReaderService.com

EXPLORE.

Sign up for the Harlequin e-newsletter and download a free book from any series at **TryHarlequin.com.**

CONNECT.

Join our Harlequin community to share your thoughts and connect with other romance readers!
Facebook.com/groups/HarlequinConnection

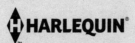

H HARLEQUIN®

**ROMANCE WHEN
YOU NEED IT**

HSOCIAL2018